"I KNEW YOU'D FEEL
LIKE THIS IN MY ARMS."

His mouth brushed her closed lids. "God help me.
. . . I wanted this the moment I saw you. It was there in
your eyes . . . the promise of gentleness and warmth. Sweet
heaven, I've been cold for so long . . . so damned long."

Apparently he took her stillness to mean acceptance.
She felt a feathering of sensation against her flesh as if
from a warm wind long before she was even aware of
his lowering head. Biting her teeth viciously into her
lower lip, she jerked her head aside, trying to hold on
to her sanity against the furious assault of his marauding
mouth. . . .

FOREVER EDEN

Noelle Berry McCue

A CANDLELIGHT ECSTASY ROMANCE ™

Published by
Dell Publishing Co., Inc.
1 Dag Hammarskjold Plaza
New York, New York 10017

To my parents, Herman and Della,
who comfort me with their love,
and strengthen me with their faith.

Dell ® TM 681510, Dell Publishing Co., Inc.

Candlelight Ecstasy Romance™ is a trademark of Dell Publishing
Co., Inc., New York, New York.

ISBN: 0–440–12619–3

Printed in the United States of America

First printing—October 1982

To Our Readers:

We have been delighted with your enthusiastic response to Candlelight Ecstasy Romances and we thank you for the interest you have shown in this exciting series.

In the upcoming months, we will continue to present the distinctive, sensuous love stories you have come to expect only from Ecstasy. We look forward to bringing you many more books from your favorite authors and also the very finest work from new authors of contemporary romantic fiction.

As always, we are striving to present the unique, absorbing love stories that you enjoy most—books that are more than ordinary romance.

Your suggestions and comments are always welcome. Please write to us at the address below.

Sincerely,

The Editors
Candlelight Romances
1 Dag Hammarskjold Plaza
New York, New York 10017

CHAPTER ONE

Rain poured from a leaden sky, quickly soaking everyone out in it through and through. As Eden McAllister walked from the air-conditioned confines of the plane to the relative security of the airport terminal, depression dogged each squishy footstep. This was all she needed to set the seal on a long and tiring day, she thought.

With renewed determination she fought her way through the jostling crowds and into the building, breathing a quick sigh of relief at finally escaping the huge, pelting drops outside. A small smile tugged at the corner of her mouth as her sparkling brown eyes observed a scene of bustling activity. Never down for long, she could feel her spirits rising with the multitude of sights and sounds around her.

Excitement pervaded the atmosphere of the Redding airport, and she responded to its call with an excitement of her own. New people and places always had this effect on her, but never more so than now. For the first time in her career as an architect she was going to be completely on her own, and the thought was a heady one.

Approaching the long counter with renewed confidence, she smiled at the man perched behind its laminated surface, receiving an insultingly brief smile in return. He returned to shuffling the papers in front of him, and Eden nearly laughed aloud, well used to being ignored by the male of the species. With her medium length, mousy brown hair curling in wayward disobedience, tip-tilted nose with a smattering of freckles, she knew she was nothing to write home about. Unclothed, her figure was daintily curved in all the right places, but the bored young man stifling a yawn had no way of knowing that, she thought, with irrepressible mirth.

"Excuse me," she persisted, her voice softly melodious but carrying very little power when it came to getting attention. As she expected, the sandy-haired, pudgy youth ignored her, and she once again felt a familiar sense of irritation at her inability to command notice. Clearing her throat more loudly than necessary, she gave a beaming smile to help counteract the rudeness of his behavior.

"May I help you?"

About time, she thought, holding the smile with effort. "I'm expecting to be met by my employer," she murmured. "My name's Eden McAllister. Have there been any messages for me?"

He emitted a voluble sigh, and Eden had to prevent herself from gritting her teeth at the sound. He looked down at the watch on his wrist, his sandy brows almost meeting with the intensity of his frown.

"Just a minute and I'll check," he ordered, shrugging his shoulders while getting to his feet with maddening slowness.

While she waited for his return, Eden studied the people around her. She could almost tell which were tourists from their mode of dress. There was a plethora of Western garb, and she was amused to notice the large, brimmed hats perched snugly upon heads which completed the image. Women were dressed in everything from floral dresses to jeans and scanty tops which bared their midriffs, and as she listened to the renewed ferocity of the rain on the roof of the terminal, she shuddered in sympathy. She hadn't counted on early spring being quite this wet either, she thought, hugging her lightweight linen coat tighter around her clammy flesh.

Eden jumped, turning at the sound of her name being spoken, and almost gasped aloud at the sight of the toothy smile on the face of the obnoxious young man from behind the counter.

"Yes?"

"Miss McAllister," he repeated. "Mr. Lassiter has requested you to take a taxi to Lassiter House. He sends his apologies, but it seems the rain caused some serious drainage problems, and he had to be on hand to supervise the work. You'll find the taxi waiting out front."

"My luggage . . ."

"That's all been taken care of," he remarked, a fatuous expression on his face. "When Mr. Lassiter makes arrangements, things get done."

"I don't see why," she argued, resisting the urge to slap the silly grin from his face. "He's just a man like any other."

"Ahhh, I can see you've never met your employer," he nodded, curiosity rampant in his closely spaced eyes.

Eden didn't bother to reply, not wanting to encourage gossip, especially with this particularly unlikable person. Turning with a vague "thank you," she headed for the glass doors, grimacing as they opened, and she was struck with whipping moisture precipitated by a bitter wind.

The taxi driver seemed to know where they were going better than she did, so she left him alone. Visibility was almost nil, and she sat back with a resigned sigh. A vague odor of damp leather mingled with another, stronger smell, one she was certain emanated from the silent driver, and she wrinkled her nose with distaste.

Within a short space of time they turned off of the main highway, and as the road twisted upward, she tensed. A sickness invaded her stomach, and she clenched her hands tightly together in her lap. Time spun viciously backward, and she closed her eyes against the agony of memory. She once again heard the sound of crunching metal, her inner eye registering her thoughts with horrifying detail. She remembered the disbelieving terror on John's face as the car slid over the edge, his last minute attempt to protect them with his body. . . .

She must have moaned aloud, for the driver's voice pierced the nightmare.

"Are you all right, lady?"

Pulling her hair back from her face with a shaking hand, she mumbled a reassurance, although it was evident from his expression the driver didn't believe her. She resisted the urge to scream at him to watch where he was going, turning her head to face the welcome breeze after rolling down the window.

"Listen, lady. If you're going to be sick, I could pull over," he muttered nervously, his eyes taking in the whiteness of the face once again turned in his direction.

"No . . . really," she protested, a strained smile curving a mouth as gently formed as a child's. "I'm fine."

"Well, if you're sure," he said, his tone doubtful as he negotiated another turn. "If you change your mind . . ."

Eden gave the driver what she hoped was a reassuring smile, although after catching sight of her ashen face in the rearview mirror she very much doubted it. Words were beyond her, and she surreptitiously wiped the tiny beads of moisture from her upper lip, hoping he wouldn't notice this added indication of her distress.

In an attempt to push the painful memories aside, she made a determined effort to study the scenery they were passing. Without the fogginess of the window to cloud her vision, she was able to make out the solitary grandeur of Mount Shasta in the far distance, rising with commanding individuality as if set apart from the Sierra mountains beside it. Clad in ice and snow, the colossal cone appeared to be an unmistakable landmark, as if it were a polestar of the landscape.

Eden breathed deeply. The smell of the rain mingling with the dampened earth was pleasing, obscuring the fetid odors inside the stuffy cab. Releasing her breath on a sigh, she craned her neck upward, her eyes taking in the grandeur of the imposing conifers liberally lacing the countryside with a garland of green.

Soon the car reached the top of a rise, and she nearly gasped at the sight that met her widening eyes. Even the rain couldn't totally obliterate the impressive sight of Lake Shasta spreading curling tendrils far into the distance. Excitement caused her heartbeat to increase as she thought of her plans for the vacation property soon to be developed on the shores of the lake. She had already submitted tentative drawings and had them approved by her employer, but she wanted to see the actual property before deciding on suitable building materials.

A nature lover, she hated to see natural splendor spoiled by man's often careless hands. She specialized in building to blend rather than overshadow, and obviously her employer shared her sentiments. He had seen the last project she had assisted in on the shore of Lake Tahoe, and specifically requested either McAllister or Bradshaw, the senior architect, when contacting the firm.

It had been a lucky break for her when Henry Bradshaw was unable to work on the project, having already contracted to do a job in Phoenix. Poor Henry, he was chagrined at the missed opportunity once he realized the location, much preferring the Lake Shasta area to the arid temperatures of Arizona. Still, it was Eden's big chance to make a name for herself as an individual and not just part of a team, and no matter what it cost her, she didn't intend to blow it. Lately she had felt lost in the firm, unable to measure up to the changing demands of her profession. Architecture was a highly competitive field, and there were too many bright young men and women ready to step into the shoes of anyone unable to pull their weight. After nearly four years with Henrick and Thompson, she had begun to feel apprehensive over her lack of individual credits.

Now, thanks to Mr. Lassiter, all that was changing. His praise of her designs, drawn from aerial photographs, brought her to the attention of the head of the firm, and she would never cease to be grateful. For the first time she had been recognized by her colleagues as an important member of the team, and the sometimes envy-producing attention she had received over the last several months had been wonderful.

As if her thoughts conjured up evidence that her employer existed on something other than paper, Eden noticed a large wrought-iron design indicating Lassiter House. As the cab passed through the open gates in a high, rock wall of singular beauty, she felt nervous tension assail her. Quickly taking her brush from her purse, she attempted to restore some measure of order to her tangled hair as the cab wound upward over the smoothly paved drive.

As the cab pulled to a stop, Eden stared in awestruck delight at the house set several hundred yards distant, flanked by tall ponderosa pines, with Douglas fir and cedar mingling to enhance its beauty. Although modern in design, the long expanse of the peak-roofed structure blended naturally with its surroundings, the use of natural wood and smoked glass creating a belonging effect. The house seemed to reach out to her in welcome, and she exited the cab hurriedly, eager to enter through the high, iron-studded doors.

Animation lightened her features, causing gentle color to flood her cheeks as she turned toward the driver. He stood for a moment, staring at her in bemused surprise, before belatedly refusing the money she was holding out. Shaking his head, he assured her that the fare had already been taken care of.

Watching as the cab pulled away after the driver had kindly deposited her luggage under the gabled roof of the porch, Eden took a deep breath and turned around to face the closed doors in front of her. With a slightly unsteady hand she reached for the circular iron rung deeply embedded in the wood, lifting it and letting it drop to indicate her arrival to those inside.

"Yes?"

It wasn't only the abruptness of the question that startled her into uttering an undignified gasp, but also the presence of the man uttering it. At well over six feet, the man was huge, dwarfing her own five feet four ignominiously. Her eyes traveled upward over firmly muscled thighs in snugly fitting cords, lingering disbelievingly on

13

brawny arms exposed by the rolled-up sleeves of the checked shirt he wore.

"May I ask what you're doing here? This is private property, as the sign in the drive clearly indicates."

"I . . . I'm here to see Mr. Lassiter," she mumbled, raising frightened eyes to a harshly unwelcoming countenance.

"What do you want?"

At the rudeness of his question, Eden bristled. *What business was it of his, the big oaf!* She wasn't going to let some handyman intimidate her! "I would prefer discussing that with Mr. Lassiter himself, if you don't mind."

She had always thought hazel eyes warm until she saw his lower to embrace her slight form with chilling disdain. His expression was menacing, to say the least. She shifted her weight nervously, all at once becoming aware of the isolation of her surroundings.

"I'm Steven Lassiter," he barked, his gaze narrowing when he noticed the dismay his words evoked.

"You're . . ." she began, staring at him nonplussed. Her visions of an elderly, kindly benefactor faded with alarming abruptness, and she swallowed with difficulty.

"That's right," he reaffirmed mockingly. "I'm Steven Lassiter, and whatever game you're trying to pull, I'm not interested."

"How dare you!"

Shrugging his shoulders, a sarcastic grin split his features. "Oh, I dare, all right. Now, just go away, there's a good girl."

With his words he turned, and Eden panicked as he began closing the door in her face. "B-but you don't understand," she spluttered, her hand a puny defense upon the oaken panels. "Y-you're expecting me!"

14

"What the hell are you talking about?"

With a despairing gesture Eden's glance traveled toward her luggage, tucked away out of sight from his position in the doorway. His eyes followed the movement of her head, and as she faced him once again she saw sudden comprehension cross his chiseled features.

The virulent string of invectives that poured forth from his firmly molded lips made Eden want to place her hands over her ears. Color rising, she stood her ground until quiet once more reigned, but found she almost preferred his swearing. The look he shot her was venomous, and she could feel a slow trembling setting up a chain reaction in her stomach.

"Your name . . . or can I guess?" he demanded, his voice holding a bitter inflection Eden just didn't understand. Surely he had expected her to arrive today? Yes, she remembered the message at the airport clearly enough, and he had obviously arranged for her transportation. What, then, was the matter with the man? Had he gone completely mad?

"Eden McAllister, from the firm of Henrick and Thompson," she muttered, her tone defensive. "I believe we have some business to discuss, Mr. Lassiter, but for the life of me I can't understand your attitude. You did contract for the building of a holiday resort?"

"You'd better come in," he said, moving aside for her to enter. "I'm afraid there's been some mistake."

His words caused a cold lump of apprehension to form in her throat as she followed him through a slate-floored vestibule, its cathedral ceiling's large skylight sending prisms of dancing light across the pale gray walls. Traversing a short corridor, he led her into what was obviously a study. A huge, stone fireplace flanked by floor-to-ceiling

15

bookcases covered the far wall, with a grouping of comfortable-looking chairs set directly in front of a welcoming fire. It was in this direction he motioned for her to precede him, and she followed his silent commands with alacrity. Over the last few weeks she had pushed hard to complete the work she had on hand, just to be free to get here on time . . . and now this! After an exhausting trip, foul weather, and being faced by this angry stranger, she didn't think her legs would hold up much longer.

As soon as she had seated herself in the large, tan leather easy chair, she regretted it. He towered above her, and she resented the helpless feeling it gave her. She was at an immediate disadvantage, and from his expression, she had the sneaking suspicion he had planned her discomfort deliberately. As if that wasn't bad enough, the chair was much too large for her to sit back comfortably, and she flushed as she scooted forward to enable her feet to once again touch the shag carpeting.

"I want to know what the hell your firm was about, sending a woman for a project of this size!"

Eden forgot all about the discomfort of her body as the meaning behind his words became clear. That was why he hadn't known who she was. He thought Eden McAllister was a man!

"What difference does my sex make, Mr. Lassiter?" she questioned coldly, the hair bristling on the nape of her neck at his chauvinistic attitude. "I'm a fully qualified architect, and might I remind you that it was you yourself who specified either McAllister or Bradshaw for the job."

With a snort of disgust, he turned, presenting a formidable profile for her inspection. Raking a hand through his hair in a frustrated gesture, he stared into the flames before speaking.

"Look," he said, turning to face her once again. "I had no idea that McAllister was a woman. Hell, the name Eden's unusual enough to be taken for a man's name. The mistake was a stupid one on my part, although understandable enough."

"I still don't see what difference it makes!"

"I'll tell you, shall I?" Eden didn't like the sneer in his voice, but decided to let it pass. There was enough antagonism in the air without adding any more, and she wanted this job desperately.

"All right," she sighed, clasping her hands together in her lap. "I'm listening."

"This area is isolated, Miss McAllister," he began, at last seating himself in the chair opposite hers. "I would expect you to live here, in my home. Is my meaning clear enough?"

The idea of living in the same house as this man didn't appeal much to Eden, but she would live with the devil himself if it meant completing the months of hard work she had already put into this project.

"We're living in the twentieth century, Mr. Lassiter, and I'm a grown woman, not a young girl afraid for her virtue. Frankly, I still don't see where my presence would cause an insurmountable problem."

"I have a ten-year-old daughter," he retorted. "Does that answer your question?"

"But surely there's somewhere close to the site where I could stay? It wouldn't have to be much," she pleaded, noting his implacable expression.

"I'm afraid it's out of the question," he said, getting to his feet in a gesture of finality. "They'll just have to send someone else out to supervise the building."

"Please, y-you're not being fair," she stammered, also

rising to her feet until she stood facing him. "Those designs were mine, no one else's. I've put in months of hard work, and now you expect me to just step down and allow someone else to take over? Well, I won't do it, Mr. Lassiter. I won't!"

"I don't see that you have much choice."

"I . . . I'll sue," she threatened, fighting back tears of anger.

At her threat his face hardened perceptively. Thickly lashed lids lowered over eyes so opaque a hazel as to appear piercing in their scrutiny of her desperate features. With a sinking sensation, Eden realized her tactical error in threatening this man. Too late to do much about her unruly words, she tilted her chin defiantly in a belated attempt to stand behind her warning.

If anything, his face hardened even more, until his tanned features resembled a mask chiseled from granite. There didn't appear to be one ounce of pity within him for her plight. The momentary gleam in his eyes seemed to portray a subtle pleasure, as if he were deriving satisfaction from the situation.

"Do you think you're so valuable to your firm that they would back you in a lawsuit if it meant losing out on a commission of this size, Miss McAllister?"

His logic was irrefutable, and at his question Eden felt the hopelessness of her situation. The idea of appealing to this man's kinder instincts galled her, but if it meant being able to continue with her project, then she'd just have to swallow her pride, she decided painfully.

"Mr. Lassiter, please," she begged, lowering her eyes from the derision she glimpsed in his. "I've worked hard to get where I am. This job means everything to me. I promise you I'll do things to your satisfaction, as well or better than any man in the firm."

"I don't doubt your talents in giving satisfaction," he drawled, his eyes roaming with clear precision over her, "but I'm not biting, honey."

"H-how dare you!" Eden jumped to her feet, clenching her fists to prevent herself from slugging him. "You h-have no right to infer—"

"That you'd do just about anything to keep this commission?"

Eden stared at him out of haunted brown eyes, feeling as if she'd just been hit below the belt. He was hateful . . . disgusting!

"Well, am I right?" Once again his cold gaze raked her shaking form, searing her with the force of the man's personality. Wordless, she could only stare at the burnished copper of his hair, unable to find sufficient strength to defend herself against his allegations. Unwillingly, she felt his masculine aura surrounding her, and she wanted to cry out against the unfairness of an attraction she didn't want to feel.

"Oh, God," he muttered in disgust. "When all else fails, a woman uses tears every time!"

"I—I'm not," she protested, his words serving to give her the strength of will to push the offensive moisture back behind closed lids.

"Look, this isn't getting us anywhere," he muttered, getting to his feet and dwarfing her. "I'll call Mr. Henrick tonight and explain that I prefer a man for the job. I promise you there'll be no reflection on your capabilities. I'm sure I can make it clear to him that my decision is based only on my own personal idiosyncrasies."

"Y-you're not being at all reasonable," she cried, forcing herself to meet his eyes. "No matter what you tell him, it will appear as if I'm at fault! Don't you understand? Just give me a chance to prove myself, is that too much to ask?"

As she had suspected, her appeal had little or no effect. Before she had even finished speaking, he was shaking his head in a negative gesture, his mouth a thin, implacable line.

"This discussion is useless, Miss McAllister. My mind's made up, so we'll talk no more about it!"

Ignoring his demand, she cried, "What do you have against me?"

His sigh was more a nonverbal expression of his exasperation with her persistence than an expulsion of breath.

"Why does my decision have to be personal?"

Eden hated having a question countered with another question, but hid her annoyance admirably. Taking a deep breath, she decided to answer with honesty.

"Because I can feel your dislike," she admitted, watching for a reaction to her words. To her disappointment, he remained impassive, giving her no indication as to whether or not her remark had hit home.

"Since you seem unwilling to let things lie and retreat gracefully, you leave me with no alternative, Miss McAllister," he said, placing his large, long-fingered hands on his hips in a belligerent stance. "Women serve me occasionally. I'm a man, after all, but as far as having one around on a more or less permanent basis, I draw the line."

"Mr. Lassiter, if I were some kind of femme fatale I could understand your reasoning, but I'm not, and have no desire to be. All I want to do is complete the job I've started. Look, I'm sure we could come to some kind of

20

amicable arrangement, if that's your only objection," she said, eagerness and renewed hope lightening her features. "I'm certain I could find accommodation in Redding. I'll hire or lease a car to get me back and forth, and you won't have to worry about your neighbors making assumptions about my living in your home. Don't you think that would work out?"

A large hand slammed against the stone fireplace, causing Eden to jump nervously. Staring at the growing anger on his face, all hope for being able to work something out with the chauvinistic male standing in front of her fled.

"Damn it, if that was the only reason for my decision, you could live in the cabin my daughter and I shared while I was building this place," he retorted, running a hand violently through the thickness of his hair. "I just don't want you here, and I don't feel I can make it any plainer than that!"

Eden hoped her features didn't show the hurt his decision had caused. Clinging to whatever pride she had left, she said, "I'm sorry for taking up so much of your time, Mr. Lassiter. Would you mind calling me a cab? I'm rather tired, and want to check into a motel as soon as possible."

"That won't be necessary," he remarked, turning from his contemplation of the fire to face her. "There's a convention in town. I doubt you'll find any accommodations. You'll have to spend the night here, and in the morning the cab can take you directly to the airport."

A throbbing ache pounded her temples, the strain of the last hour having crumpled her confidence to the degree that she didn't feel capable of arguing with this formidable stranger, and with dragging feet she followed him from the room.

CHAPTER TWO

Lassiter House was everything a house should be. The L-shaped structure was spacious without being at all pretentious, the use of natural wood and glass blending into a pleasing whole. Polished wood floors, flagstone hallways, and light wall tones mingled to create a warmth often missing in large houses. Although finding her surroundings perfect, once alone in the farthest wing, a frustrating sense of disappointment settled over Eden like a pall.

Plopping onto a chaise longue with her feet curled beneath her, she stared at what she was sure would have been her quarters, and sighed. The sitting room, with bedroom and bath beyond, was furnished neutrally, its fittings neither masculine nor feminine. Like the rest of the house she had seen so far, these rooms echoed warmth, and she couldn't help wondering how this could have been achieved by a man as cold as Steven Lassiter.

But was cold really the appropriate word to use in connection with the person she had just met? she wondered. Remembering the full sensuality of his mouth, the aura of rugged vitality that had seemed to surround her when in his presence, however unwillingly, she somehow doubted he was as cold as he wanted her to believe.

No! For some reason the man was eaten up with bitterness toward women. She suddenly felt nothing but pity for his young daughter. From what she gathered, there wasn't a wife in the picture, and a young girl on the threshold of womanhood wasn't going to find it easy growing up.

Exhaustion was catching up with her, and Eden curled into a more comfortable position on the chaise. Facing the sliding glass doors, she drowsily tried to penetrate the early evening darkness, but was unable to see anything but her own reflection. She looked like a child, huddled defensively on the chaise, her curly brown hair framing the smallness of her face in tangled disarray.

She must have dozed for a moment, because the next thing of which she was conscious was opening her eyes to see a child standing quietly in front of her. Something told her to remain as still as possible, some hidden intuition, and silently she inspected the child while a slow pain tore through her.

Long, blond hair hung down her back in snarls, framing a thin, pinched, little face. But it was the eyes that disturbed Eden most. Large, rounded orbs in a clear, piercing blue. They were Shelley's eyes . . . her Shelley. Oh, God! she thought, fighting to hold back a groan. Shelley . . . Shelley . . .

For long, tense moments she devoured the little girl with her gaze, shuddering with the pain of her emotions. Time seemed to stand still. She was caught in a blending maelstrom of the past and present, trapped somewhere in an isolated netherland between. This fey, haunted child was Steven Lassiter's! She must be, Eden reasoned, a sense of disbelief flooding through her.

Eden thought later that it was as if the little girl just faded away. One minute she was there, the next, gone as quietly as she had come. Pacing the room, chills coursed through her body, and she wrapped her arms tightly around herself while trying to come to grips with reality. An eerie sense of inevitability settled over her, and she bit her lip to stop herself from crying out.

Shelley would have been nearly ten had she . . . No! her mind screamed. She wouldn't remember, wouldn't deliberately resurrect the pain of her loss so many years ago. Instead she would think of this living child, this strange, silent child. There had been something unnatural in the encounter, she realized. She had sensed a distrust in the small figure, whose gaze hadn't been at all childlike. Only for a brief second had there been even a flicker of warmth in eyes chillingly cold, and it had disappeared almost instantly, leaving Eden feeling agitated and disturbed.

A knock on the door jerked her from her thoughts, and Eden opened it with trepidation.

"Dinner's ready, Miss McAllister."

"Oh, but I . . ."

"Don't tell me you're not hungry," Steven ordered, frowning down at her from his towering height. "The dining room's on your left. I'll expect you in five minutes."

Really, the man's an impossible boor, she thought. Eden closed the door on his rapidly departing figure and walked into the bathroom to wash. Of cream and gold, it wasn't as austere as most bathrooms, and she looked around her with appreciation. Drying her hands, she inspected her face for signs of wear, and cringed at her appearance. With determination she went into the bedroom where her luggage had been deposited in a transitory heap.

Returning to the bathroom with her makeup case, she decided to start with attempting to instill some order into her hair. Not long enough to pin up, she had to settle for a quick brushing, once again glaring at the childish image reflected in the glass. She never wore much makeup, but tonight she decided on a pale-green eyeshadow and blusher for her pale cheeks.

Her oyster linen shirtwaist dress wasn't what she would have chosen for dinner with the imposing Steven Lassiter, but it would have to do. Although she would have preferred a change of clothes, there wasn't time, and, anyway, she thought wryly, her appearance wouldn't change his opinion of her one bit.

She remembered passing the open double doors of the dining room when he was showing her to her room, and this gave her the confidence to walk down the long hallway with her inner nervousness well hidden. The first thing she noticed when entering was the room's emptiness. Was she to have dinner alone, in isolated splendor? she wondered almost hopefully. Her eyes turned to the table, but she knew the hope was dashed when she spotted two place settings.

"I see you found it all right," a masculine voice sounded from behind her.

Whirling around, her large eyes expressive of her startled awareness, she muttered an affirmative.

With a coolly polite smile he guided her to her place at the table, and Eden could feel herself trembling as she sat down. Furious with herself for being unable to find anything to say, she sat in uncomfortable silence. With a sense of relief she heard footsteps behind her coming from the direction of the kitchen. An older woman entered pushing a trolley, and Eden smiled as she stopped beside her chair.

Seeing the silent exchange, Steven Lassiter introduced Eden to Mrs. Adams, a neighbor whose husband, he explained grudgingly, handled the upkeep of the massive grounds of the estate.

"I'm happy to meet you, Mrs. Adams," Eden said, and the woman's ample form straightened in surprised pleasure.

"You don't know how happy I am to see someone like you around," she replied cryptically, sending Steven a speaking glance from beneath lowered lids.

Puzzled, Eden glanced in his direction. She saw his eyes sparkle dangerously in the tightness of his face as he looked at the other woman. There was a nerve-wracking moment of silence, and Eden could almost feel the increased tension in the suddenly stifling room.

"That will be all, Mrs. Adams," he said, his words clearly dismissing the other woman. "We'll serve ourselves."

As she departed, the housekeeper gave a disparaging sniff.

"Well?" Steven intoned.

The question held a dry inflection which made Eden bristle defensively. Refusing to answer, she struggled to outstare him, only to lower her eyes in defeat in an ignominiously short space of time.

"Aren't you going to question me about Mrs. Adams's presence?"

"Should I?"

Her reply was as taunting as his question. With a defensive tilting of her rounded chin, she waited for what she knew would be another scathing remark. To her surprise he looked almost confused by her attitude, and she had to forcibly restrain herself from squirming under the hooded intensity of his stare.

"I assumed you'd use the fact that I do allow a woman

to serve as my housekeeper to launch another argument in your defense."

Eden studied the features of this self-contradictory man in bewilderment. If she didn't know better, she'd think he was deliberately trying to provoke another confrontation. That didn't even make sense, unless he enjoyed seeing her beg. As soon as the thought crossed her mind, she felt it was the right one. She was an insect on a pin to this man, someone to vent his macho ego upon, but she wasn't about to give him the satisfaction. She knew when she was butting her head against a brick wall. Didn't she still feel a dull throbbing from the last incident?

Eden had quietly been applying herself to sipping a delicious concoction of vegetables and broth, as she was hungrier than she'd at first realized, when she heard Steven utter a choked gasp.

When she had first begun eating, she questioned the absence of his daughter at the table, and he had told her she disliked strangers, and would eat in her room. Her presence now, standing silently beside Eden's chair, gave lie to his assertion, but from the white-faced shock creasing his features, she presumed this occurrence was far from ordinary.

Turning her head and seeing the child for the first time in full light, Eden just barely stopped herself from uttering a gasp. Still dressed in faded jeans and a soiled T-shirt, the little girl just looked at Eden as if searching her eyes.

Indulging in her own search of the small features, she smiled gently, afraid of startling this petite creature. To her delight a fleeting answer curved the rosebud mouth. Another strangled gasp rent the stillness from Steven Lassiter's direction, and Eden turned toward him in shocked inquiry.

28

"That was my daughter," he whispered, staring at the doorway through which the child had fled. "Her name is Dawn."

"Did I frighten her away?" Eden's distress was unfeigned as she turned disturbed eyes in his direction.

"Frighten her?" His words were enunciated slowly, as if his mind were involved with a weightier problem. "I'm still trying to figure out what in the hell made her show herself at all!"

"Were you deliberately trying to keep her away from me?" Eden demanded, before she could stop herself.

Instead of the anger she expected, she saw genuine wonderment in the eyes that turned to study her indignant features. "No," he murmured, shaking his head and leaning back in his chair. Until that moment Eden hadn't been aware of the tenseness in his large frame, and as he again applied himself to his dinner, she realized she wasn't going to get any clearer an explanation for his strange behavior.

She picked at the salad and roast beef he handed her, her appetite submerged in anger. She was normally a gentle-natured creature, hating discord of any kind, and the emotions this man aroused in her left her feeling unable to cope. She wasn't used to being anything other than self-effacing, probably the greatest reason she hadn't risen in her chosen career at the rate of her abilities. Although she often wished for a brasher, more outgoing personality, she couldn't seem to change her overly shy nature, and as a result was generally overlooked. Why, then, did she find herself in danger of behaving like an undersized amazon with Mr. Bighead Lassiter? she wondered.

Eden still hadn't come up with any satisfactory conclusions by the time she went to bed. She hadn't stayed in his presence for any longer than it took her to finish the meal,

29

but it was as if his aura followed her through the confusion of her thoughts. She couldn't seem to get him and his daughter off her mind, and even a shower hadn't helped to alleviate the strange tension gripping her.

The comfortable warmth of the bed soon seduced her into a more relaxed state of mind, and sleep overcame her. Deeper and deeper she wandered through pleasant mists of slumber, until a small sound penetrated her consciousness. Opening her eyes, she noticed the indistinct shape of a man standing over her, the strange glint in his eyes made visible by the light filtering from the hallway. Sheer terror seized her, a fear so great she couldn't even utter the scream she felt building deep inside her trembling body.

Clutching the sheet defensively against the sheerness of her nightgown, she sat up, only then noticing a curled shadow on the coverlet at her feet. She watched through widening eyes as Steven bent down, his arms gentle as he cradled the sleeping girl in his arms. Moving with surprising lightness for such a large man, he left the room. Staring at the closing door, Eden drew her breath on a shaky sigh, the incident taking on the dimensions of a dream. As she once again drifted into sleep, she wondered if everything she thought she had seen had really been a figment of her imagination, especially the look of intense pain on Steven Lassiter's face.

Early the next morning Eden half-pushed, half-carried her luggage across the hall, determined to manage without the help of the master of the house. She had dressed in serviceable brown denims and a burnt-orange madras blouse for the occasion of her departure, no longer caring whether or not she created a businesslike image.

Strangely enough, the hallway seemed much longer

than it had last night. Pausing momentarily, she pressed her palm against the small of her back, blowing a recalcitrant lock of hair from her perspiring forehead in exasperation.

"What in hell do you think you're doing?"

"Do you have to creep up on me like that?" Eden sent a fulminating glare in the direction of the man just coming into the hall from the entryway. "You must enjoy seeing me jump."

"You didn't answer my question."

"I should think the answer is obvious," she retorted, disgust at the untimely interruption coating her voice. "If you'll call that cab, I'll remove my unwelcome presence from your house, Mr. Lassiter."

"No!"

Eden felt as if she had taken all she could from this brute of a man. So far she'd managed to control her emotions, but for the sake of her sanity she was going to have to lose her composure in a minute. Although rarely showing itself, she did possess a temper, and by the pounding of her heart she recognized that her anger was about to override her timidity.

A slow smile creased Steven's face as he watched the conflicting emotions chasing themselves across her features.

"You look as if you're ready to explode!"

His words burst in her brain with sickening force, and before she felt her feet moving, she was standing close to him, her head tilted back in an effort to meet his mockingly hateful eyes.

"You . . . you ba—"

"Now, now," he soothed, his hand reaching out to

31

grasp her wrist in steely fingers. "Don't you know better than to use a word like that? It isn't very ladylike."

"What game are you playing now, Mr. Lassiter?"

"Believe me," he replied grimly, pulling her in the direction of the study. "I wish it were a game."

Why do I behave like a damn mouse? she thought, disgusted with herself for allowing him to drag her along behind him as if she were a lamb being led to the slaughter. Indeed, the way her wrist ached from the pressure of his fingers, she wondered if this madman did have intentions along those lines.

"Sit down," he ordered, releasing her and closing the doors to the study.

She wanted to stick her tongue out at him, but she decided to settle for a haughty silence. She was certain that after her unconventional entry into the room, she could never manage anything more dignified!

He had placed her in a chair beside a massive oak desk which covered nearly a quarter of one wall, and then perched himself upon the edge of it, much too close for comfort. She would have preferred him to seat himself behind the desk, like any self-respecting ex-employer, but she didn't have the courage to utter the protest. *That's what it amounts to,* she thought, *a lack of guts.* That wasn't the most ladylike term either, but it certainly fit her imagery appropriately!

". . . so what it boils down to is, you'll be staying for a couple of days."

Eden looked up at him in bewilderment, belatedly realizing that she had missed the whole point of the conversation. She had been so busy castigating herself, she hadn't heard a word he was saying. Did this mean he was reconsidering, giving her a couple of days to prove herself?

Uttering the question with bated breath, her heart sank when she observed the disgusted expression on his face.

"Didn't you hear a word I said?"

"Only the last part," she admitted, feeling a flush creep up her face. She hated it when she blushed, knowing how it made the freckles spattered across the bridge of her diminutive nose stand out. Obviously he noticed, because a mocking gleam darkened the depths of his eyes, causing her blush to deepen.

Tiring of deriding her with his stare, he uttered an exasperated sigh before delving into another explanation. Apparently the rain had caused problems at the airport, and she wouldn't be able to get a flight out until Monday. The convention members were also locked into Redding, so her chances of finding other accommodation were no better than they had been the night before.

"Look, I have no intention of staying here another hour, much less a whole weekend," she retorted, rising to her feet in her agitation. "I'm sure I can find somewhere to stay in town."

"Don't you think I've already tried," he replied dampeningly, swinging one long leg indolently as he uttered the words.

He certainly doesn't believe in flattering a girl, she thought, feeling little humor at the idea. He was leaving her with no doubt that he had tried to be rid of her at the first opportunity. Well, so be it! She didn't care if she had to sleep on a park bench, she wasn't going to inflict herself on him any longer. Telling him as much, although her natural good manners took the edge off her words somewhat, she was appalled by the derisive quirk to his firmly molded lips.

"You echo my sentiments exactly, Miss McAllister.

Mrs. Adams is in the process of cleaning out that cabin I mentioned last night. I'm sure you'll be able to tolerate the isolation for a couple of nights."

He certainly had the ability to take the wind out of her sails, she thought with a great degree of exasperation. Even though she wanted alternative accommodations, his mention of isolation caused her to pause, a frisson of unease coursing through her.

"Just how isolated is this place?" she squeaked, her eyes widening in alarm. She knew from experience just how dark the nights could be in this area from her brief foray of the terrace outside her sitting room the night before. She had barely been able to see her hand in front of her face.

"I'm afraid it's located at the bottom of the road," he replied, his expression smug. "Any complaints?"

Even if she had had any, she wouldn't have voiced them after hearing that self-satisfied note in his voice. Obviously he expected her to retreat from his suggestion in fright, but he could just think again, she vowed silently. She might be a timid person by nature, and a coward where people were concerned, but she wasn't afraid to stay alone, even in the midst of a wilderness if need be!

"I think I'll be quite happy in your cabin, Mr. Lassiter," she said. Looking into his eyes, she observed a spark lightening their depths, of, could it be, grudging admiration.

"That's fine," he replied, moving to his feet with fluid grace. "I'll show you the place as soon as you've had breakfast. In the meantime, Joe Adams will take your bags over."

"Thank you," she muttered, edging backward slightly to escape the warmth emanating from his blue Pendleton-shirted figure. A mocking gesture of his hand advised her

34

to precede him from the study, and she managed to exit the room without embarrassing herself by tripping on her rather unsteady legs.

She was relieved to find he had already eaten. She didn't think she could stand choking down another meal in his presence. He led her to a tiny breakfast alcove which was flooded with bright morning sunlight from recessed greenhouse windows. He only grunted unintelligibly when she expressed her admiration, and she pressed her lips together at his rudeness to stop herself from becoming equally rude.

The meal was extremely satisfying, and she was pleasantly sated after devouring scrambled eggs in cheese sauce, three slices of toast, and a disgusting number of sausages. The meal had been waiting for her under a warmed cover, and she indulged herself with pleasure as soon as Steven left the room. Although small and thin, Eden was often embarrassed by her voracious appetite, especially when in the company of a man. Not that she had been in the habit of eating with many men since John
. . .

Not wanting to further those thoughts, she wiped her mouth with the linen napkin in her lap and rose to her feet. She would have loved another cup of Mrs. Adams's delicious coffee, but, looking down at her wristwatch, she decided she had wasted enough of the morning. She couldn't wait to get outside and explore this area she would be able to enjoy for such a short time. Although a city girl, she loved the outdoors with passionate intensity. Every chance she got she headed for the beaches near her apartment, or into the mountains whenever possible.

A brisk wind buffeted her as soon as she stepped out onto the porch, but it wasn't cold. Bright sunlight sparkled freely, soaking into the still-damp earth. Taking a deep breath of the clear air, she raised her face toward the golden orb in the sky. She couldn't believe the difference in the clarity of the sky compared to smog-laden Los Angeles.

"Are you ready to go?"

Turning to face Steven, Eden's heart sank when she noticed the scowl on his face. What in the world was he angry about now? As far as she was aware, she'd done nothing more to incur his wrath. Surely he didn't resent the fact that she was enjoying the pleasant aspects of his property without seeking his permission?

"Do I look as if I'm chained to the ground?"

An annoying smirk creased the corners of his mouth. "No, but I was beginning to think you were chained to the breakfast table," he mocked.

Eden pressed her lips together to prevent herself from making the retort in her mind. It was just like the man to notice her lengthy consumption of breakfast, she thought, beginning to stiffly march down the graveled path, not caring if he followed. She wouldn't have been a bit surprised if he had gone back to check on the quantities of food missing from the serving dishes!

"You eat a lot for such a scrawny woman," he continued outrageously. "When I look at you, I'm reminded of a little brown doe. They eat voraciously directly after the mating season to nourish their growing young. You're not by any chance . . . ?"

Eden felt as if she were burning alive, and not just with embarrassment. It was almost as though something foreign to her nature was slowly taking control. She hardly recognized herself around this aggravating man. She was sure she had never before experienced the gamut of emotional conflict she had suffered since arriving in this paradise. Maybe her name was apt after all, she thought, turning long enough to glare into his amused eyes. Well, if her name was apt, his certainly wasn't. He should be called Serpent instead of Steven!

They reached the end of the road in silence, with Steven guiding her onto an adjacent footpath. If he hadn't been with her, she probably would have missed it, it had become so overgrown. Trees thickened, meeting overhead and blocking out the warmth, and Eden shivered. For some reason she didn't like this place nearly as much as she had hoped she would. It was wild and quite beautiful —but forbidding. Maybe it was the wildness she distrusted. Glancing nervously around her at the dripping foliage, she noticed a plethora of twisted manzanita, and what she thought was mountain mahogany, but the predominant greenery consisted of Ponderosa pines and red and white fir trees.

Eden was thankful when the thick growth opened up into a small clearing, a rude wooden structure nestling in its center. From the way it was built, she guessed, it consisted of an open-structured central living area . . . and little else. She just hoped there wasn't an outhouse in the back! It would be just like the man at her side to spring something like that on her without warning.

"Think you can stand it?"

His voice was an infuriating drawl as he looked at her from the corner of his eye, but Eden wasn't about to let him know how frightened she was at the idea of staying all alone out here.

"I love it," she retorted, her tone belligerent. His only reply was a booming laugh at her expense.

CHAPTER THREE

It was nearly dark, and Eden's earlier nervousness had nearly vanished. Upon entering the cabin after breakfast, she had been pleasantly surprised by the coziness of the small building. She instantly fell in love with the stone fireplace, latticed windows, and natural wood floors. She had sent a beaming glance in Steven's direction, almost forgetting her earlier animosity. He hadn't let her forget for long though. After staring at her for several seconds, he had frowned, his displeasure with her contentment evident. In fact, she remembered, for a moment he had looked quite ferocious. The memory caused her to chuckle as she stacked her dinner dishes in the small but compact sink above the rickety cabinets.

Turning the tap, the smile left Eden's face. She struggled with the cold water nozzle, but nothing, absolutely nothing, happened. "Great!" she muttered. What in the world was she going to do with no water? A suspicious thought briefly crossed her mind. Before he had left, Steven had been fiddling with something under the sink. Sure, there'd been water enough to brew a pot of coffee, but couldn't that have been standing in the pipes? He wouldn't have tried to prove his point by switching off her water, surely?

Well, she wouldn't give him the satisfaction of any complaints. In the morning she would ask Mr. Adams about fixing the pipes. It would serve Nasty Lassiter right if his employee did discover the lines had been fooled with. Thoughts of Steven's embarrassment miraculously restored Eden's spirits. She wouldn't die of thirst before morning, and she had showered before attempting to drag her luggage down the hall earlier today. She'd survive!

She was still smiling when she donned her sheer nightgown. Somehow the frothy creation didn't exactly suit her setting, she thought, glancing down at the barely hidden curves of her figure. Scrawny, indeed! He would never call her *that* again if he could see her . . .

What in the world was she doing, she thought, aghast at the direction her mind was traveling. She couldn't stand the man! What ever possessed her to think in those terms about someone she despised? Searching frantically, Eden pulled a voluminous robe from her suitcase. She felt slightly better after it was buttoned up to her throat, as if the motion of her shaking fingers would serve to button up her thoughts as easily.

A log in the fireplace dropped with a shower of sparks, making a convenient focal point for her wandering attention. Walking across the floor, her canvas shoes still on her feet, she placed the fireguard more securely in front of the fire. Arms over her head in a languid stretch, she sighed, smothering a yawn unsuccessfully.

It was still too early to go to sleep, but the idea of snuggling beneath the comforter of the double bed was inviting. She would turn on the lantern-shaped lamp overhead, she thought. That should give her enough light to read by for an hour or so. With this thought in mind she extracted a book from her suitcase that she had wanted to read for ages before turning off all the other lights.

This is pure bliss, she thought, curling her toes pleasurably beneath the covers. The fire crackled merrily, and outside she could hear the faint whisper of the wind through the trees mingling with the gentle calls of the nocturnal denizens of the wilderness. Well, maybe not wilderness, she thought, smiling at the fanciful thought. Although it certainly seemed that way to her.

"What the . . ."

If it hadn't been for the glowing embers of the fire in the hearth, Eden wouldn't have even been able to see her way to the wall switch. Gritting her teeth with annoyance, she traversed the distance and . . . nothing! First the water and now no electricity, she fumed. Mr. Steven Lassiter was going to make sure she ran all the way into Redding eager for the next flight out of here. Well, she'd show him, she promised silently, fumbling in the dimness for her shoes. If he thought he was going to get away with playing these kinds of childish pranks without being told what she thought of him, he was in for a surprise!

She had seen a flashlight in the kitchen drawer while preparing her dinner. She just hoped the batteries still worked. She couldn't chance waiting until her anger cooled down, she thought, a sigh of satisfaction whistling through her clenched teeth as her hand curled around the object of her search.

Flicking the flashlight on, she nearly shook with revengeful glee. The light wasn't the brightest, but it would do to get her up the hill. Checking to see that all the buttons were fastened on her robe, she headed for the door. The robe was probably warmer than her coat anyway, reaching as it did to her ankles, and there weren't any neighbors close enough to gossip about her nocturnal wanderings.

Many times during that long walk in the pitch black of the forest Eden regretted her impetuosity. If she directed the light outward to enable her to see whether or not she was about to be eaten alive by a bear, she tripped on hidden roots. After the third painful sprawl on the hard ground, she decided it might be better to provide a satisfying meal for some animal than to lacerate her knees any further. So with the light illuminating the path, she suffered instead from her imagination. Every sound made the hair stand up on the back of her neck. She felt as if hundreds of eyes watched her slow progress. Choking down sobs of fright, she was unable to prevent slow tears from running down her cheeks.

If she hadn't already come halfway, she would have turned around and tried to make it back to the cabin. She'd never experienced such tremendous fear in her life before. Although she hated herself for her cowardice, telling herself over and over again that she was acting like a stupid fool, it didn't help much.

The lights were out in the big house, but by now Eden was beyond caring whom she disturbed. All she wanted was to get inside where there was safety from the hidden terrors of the darkness. Pounding with both fists on the kitchen door, she waited, her eyes huge as she glanced nervously behind her.

The door was opened without preliminary warning, plummeting her forward into muscular arms. She was a moaning, quaking mass of nervous tension by then, and all she could do when she realized the identity of the man holding her was to pound viciously on his chest. His words of protest made no sense to Eden in her hysterical state, nor did her leaden limbs want to obey her mental commands when he nearly dragged her into the warmth of the kitchen.

"You little wildcat," he muttered, attempting to encircle her flailing hands in his own. "What's the matter with you?"

"As if you didn't know," she stormed, kicking his shin with a resounding impact.

"Damn you! That hurt!" he swore, wrenching her arms painfully as he pulled her across the room. He sat on the edge of the large, oak table, pulling her struggling body forward until she was wedged between his massive, imprisoning thighs.

"Will you tell me what the hell this is all about?" His question was jerked from between clenched teeth, his face a forbidding mask.

"First you tinker with the pipes, that was bad enough . . . but the electricity!"

She thought she couldn't possibly get any angrier, until she saw the slight twitch begin to tilt one corner of his mouth. The twitch grew into a slow smile, and she shook with the force of her indignation. His eyes were leaping with repressed amusement, and she glared up at him in impotent rage.

"So, you think I'm responsible, hmmm?"

"Are you trying to deny your part in this attempt to frighten me into leaving?"

When he uttered a low growl which turned into uncontrollable laughter, she had to forcibly restrain herself from clawing at him. With her hands clenched at her sides, she surprised them both by twisting violently in an attempt to wrench herself from his clasp. To her shocked embarrassment, all the movement accomplished was a loss of balance, and she found herself plastered against the front of his shirt.

"I . . . I . . ."

She was incapable of speech, her apology lost somewhere amid new and disturbing sensations. Suddenly all the anger she had felt only moments before refocused into a trembling ache in the pit of her stomach, her nerve ends sensitized to feel only the burning imprint of his body against hers. She didn't dare raise her eyes, even when his breath feathered her hair in explanation.

"I don't blame you for thinking I had something to do with the plumbing and electrical problems, but I can assure you I would have never dreamed of using such devious methods. That cabin's not exactly in the first flush of youth, and neither is the wiring. As for the water, it's not unusual to have the pipes freeze over," he laughed with a rueful chuckle. "I told you the cabin wasn't in fit shape for company, but you chose not to believe me. Well, I'm sorry to disappoint you, honey, but I'm really not the devil incarnate. Believe me when I tell you that I have very good reasons for wanting you away from here. I took one look at those big eyes of yours, and knew you spelled trouble. Do you know what I'm trying to tell you?"

Eden swallowed past the constriction in her throat, finally finding the courage to raise her eyes. His final question had been no more than a huskily voiced whisper that, coupled with the heat from his body, left her a shaking mass of contradictory emotions. She only needed the hooded glitter of the eyes roaming her features to receive his message loud and clear, and she shook her head in disbelief.

"You need proof?"

"No, please . . ." Her whisper was lost in the open

cavern of his descending mouth. A frenzy shook her as he molded her back with his large hands, pulling her tighter against his straining body. His thrusting tongue forced her lips apart to add to the waves of sensation building within her. A sensual desire stronger than anything she had ever felt before ravaged her emotions, frightening her by its strength. Pushing against his chest with frantic effort only exhausted her to the point where her knees sagged. Leaning backward against the table surface, Steven supported her weight with his body, his hand behind her head forcing her to keep the kiss unbroken.

A low, feral groan blended with the loud thudding of her heart, a sound that indicated an animal arousal which horrified her. Although being kissed to be taught a lesson was bad enough, this was something else again. The hard tensing of his trembling frame told her better than words that he was quickly losing any objectivity he might have possessed. She could feel him turning her onto her side, his hands attacking the buttons of her robe, and she was helpless against his greater strength.

"Y-you've made your point," she gasped, clutching at his hands. "Please . . ."

With a sinking heart Eden doubted if he even heard her, so intense was his concentration on the task he had set himself. Her own desire was like a live thing inside of her, rendering her struggles ineffectual as he pushed the offending material of her robe aside. She shivered when his eyes darkened at the sight of her quaking body through the thinness of her gown.

A whimper escaped her as calloused brown fingers feathered over the creamy surface of her neck and shoulders. He was looking at her, apparently still unable to tear his eyes away, and couldn't see the trapped agony in her

45

luminous eyes. His hand moved once again, levering the thin straps aside. Eden closed her eyes, trying to blot out what was happening, desperately trying to subdue the response she could feel clawing its way to the surface.

"I knew you'd feel like this in my arms," he muttered, his mouth brushing her closed lids with feather-light precision. "God help me. . . . I wanted this the moment I saw you. It was there in your eyes . . . the promise of gentleness and warmth. Sweet heaven, I've been cold for so long . . . so damned long."

Apparently he took her stillness to mean acceptance. She felt a feathering of sensation against her flesh as if from a warm wind, long before she was even aware of his lowering head. Biting her teeth viciously into her lower lip, she jerked her head aside, trying to hold on to her sanity against the furious assault on her senses from his marauding mouth.

Opening her eyes, she gasped, trying to arch away from his possession of her flesh.

"The child," she cried, her voice sounding hoarse even to her own ears.

Thank God his body was obscuring his actions from his daughter. Turning to face the man who stared down at her, his own torment written clearly on his face, she wanted to sink through the floor in shame. If only she hadn't come here tonight, screaming like a shrew, they would have both been spared the embarrassment of this moment.

"Eden, I'm . . . I didn't mean it to go this far!"

His words seemed the final culmination of her growing humiliation, and she was unable to prevent the tears that slipped slowly from wounded eyes.

She shakily redid the buttons of her robe with Steven's help. Although she wanted to flinch away from the swift

46

capability of his touch, she made no demur. She doubted if she would have been capable of accomplishing the feat herself. She couldn't seem to stop shaking, and she bitterly resented his swift composure. Although he had raised her to a sitting position, his body still blocked hers from the little girl's eyes, a maneuver that, while showing consideration and sensitivity to her feelings, she was too resentful to fully appreciate.

"Bed, Dawn," Steven whispered, kneeling beside the child.

Dawn looked from her father to Eden, who was still perched frozen on the table. The only indication that she understood his command was a slight, negative shaking of her head.

"Is something wrong, darling?"

At the sound of his voice, Dawn's attention switched from her contemplation of Eden back to her father.

"Why's she crying? Why did you make her cry?"

"Honey, I . . ." Steven began, raising pleading eyes in Eden's direction.

Although it went against Eden's grain to help this impossible man out of an embarrassing situation, she couldn't resist the silent appeal. Anyway, although he didn't deserve her consideration, the child certainly did!

"Your father was just comforting me, Dawn," she explained, slipping from the table and joining Steven in a crouched position in front of the little girl. "I got scared walking here in the dark."

To Eden's consternation, Dawn jumped back away from both of them, a fiercely defiant gleam in her luminous blue eyes.

"I don't believe you," she screamed, shaking her head violently. "Daddy doesn't like you. He doesn't like me

47

anymore. Mommy said he hates me, and I hate him too. I hate him!"

Before they could stop her, she ran sobbing from the room. Both Eden and Steven seemed frozen, until with a choked cry, Steven followed her.

Slowly Eden rose to her feet, looking around the rustic kitchen bewilderedly. She was shaking with reaction both to Steven's earlier assault and the more recent scene with Dawn. Although decrying the evening's happenings, she still felt some measure of relief. All her earlier encounters with Dawn had led her to believe that the child might be retarded. Thank God she'd been wrong in her suspicions. She could speak, and from the intelligence in her sullen little face, Eden suspected their earlier meetings had been engineered by Dawn as something of a test for herself.

By now Eden's teeth were chattering violently. Noticing a pan on top of the modern copper range recessed into the corner, she quickly filled it. While the water heated, she searched the cupboards. They were well stocked, and she had no difficulty in locating a tea canister.

Before long she was at the kitchen table sipping the reviving drink gratefully. Cupping the steaming mug in hands hardly more steady than before, she looked toward the back door. She couldn't face leaving once again for the cabin, and yet the idea of spending the night within close proximity to Steven appalled her.

With her mind reviewing the unbelievable happenings she had just experienced, violent anger once again muddled her thoughts. How dare he treat her like some kind of a—thing. He was deliberately using the mindless attraction between them to gain his objective, and she would not let him back her into a corner! Poor little Dawn. Growing up in the household of a man who felt very little but contempt for the female of the species couldn't be easy for such a sensitive little girl. Could that be the reason for the child's disturbing attitude?

Pouring herself a second cup of tea, Eden frowned. Was she being quite fair? she wondered. Dawn had mentioned her mother. She had said her mother had told her that her father hated her. How could a woman do that to a child? Quite possibly it could be justified in the woman's mind as protection, but it was wrong to make a child doubt her own father's love.

Picturing the anguish she had glimpsed on Steven Lassiter's face as he hurried after Dawn, Eden had no doubt regarding the existence of that love. Strangely enough, those moments in his arms had hinted to her of a warmth and longing in a man trying desperately to deny his own needs. This, more than anything else, convinced her he was the kind of man capable of a tremendous amount of feeling. She shivered, the thought somehow vaguely threatening. He would demand as much as he gave, and as her thoughts delved into the possibilities of intimacy with such a man, she didn't question the reasons why her mind insisted on clinging to her earlier resentment.

"Will you go to her?"

Turning her head at the question, she nearly gasped at the ravaged appearance of the man standing in the doorway. Within the space of a few minutes, it was almost as if he had aged ten years, he looked so haggard and defeated. His face was again the cold and shuttered mask he had presented to her at their first meeting. The teasingly passionate man she had seen so briefly was gone, and in his place was someone carrying a burden almost too great to be borne. Although she wanted to hate him, she found a

49

strange pity twisting her heart, and a grudging admiration for his dignity as he asked for her help.

"Of course," she replied, assuming her own mantle of pride. "Where's her room?"

"This way," he said, walking from the kitchen and leaving her to follow. They walked the hallway silently, soon branching off into another section of the house. Although she followed, she stayed as far away from the warmth of his body as she could manage without appearing childish. If he noticed, he gave no sign, stopping outside a pair of white double doors.

Eden forced herself not to flinch when he turned in her direction, barely managing to restrain her nervousness. She waited to find out the reason for the delay, her eyes widening emotionally as he explained.

"She won't let me in," he said, his bluntly whispered words sounding toneless, dead, as if he were suppressing all emotion. "She's like her mother. Elaine was sick, always dreaming up neurotic fantasies. After Dawn was born, she blamed me for the pain of bearing her." His laughter was desolate. "She became terrified if I so much as entered her room. By the time Dawn was five years old Elaine hated her as much as she did me. That's why I could never understand why she bothered taking Dawn with her when she left."

"She took Dawn?" Eden swallowed with difficulty, appalled by the thought of such a woman having custody of her child.

Her question was answered almost before she had finished speaking, and the answer sickened her. According to Steven, Elaine's hatred of him had risen to such gigantic proportions that she had chosen the only revenge upon him that she had known would be effective.

50

He told her how long he had searched for his child, each lead turning out to be more useless than the last. She could sense from his words a portion of the terrible despair he must have felt, not knowing whether his wife, whom he knew to be disturbed mentally, would be mistreating his child.

"I eventually found them in a little town on the Oregon border," he continued, rubbing his hand tiredly along the back of his neck. "That was nearly three years ago."

"Did she relinquish custody?"

Eden flinched when Steven uttered bitter laughter.

"She didn't have to," he muttered, a look of vicious hatred in his eyes. "By the time I caught up with Elaine she was just living for the next bottle, and Dawn was like a little savage, undernourished and full of anger toward all adults. It's taken me three years just to get her to the point of not cowering whenever I get near her," he concluded harshly.

Now Eden knew the reason for Steven's attitude toward women, and she wished to God she didn't. She felt sickened by his disclosures, a wrenching agony of empathy radiating toward this justifiably bitter man.

"Where is Elaine now?"

Steven flinched at her question, sagging limply against the wall. "I received notification of her death six months after the custody trial. She was driving under the influence, and her car went over an embankment. God help me," he whispered, his gaze turned inward, his face registering self-disgust. "She was the mother of my child, and yet all I could feel was relief. Does that make me the monster she thought me?"

The question was pitiful, and Eden was quick to utter

a denial. "What happened when Dawn heard of her mother's death?"

"What do you think happened?" he replied, his voice conveying a wealth of weary cynicism. "She became hysterical, blaming me for everything. God! I'll never forget how she fought me, desperate to escape the torment I was inflicting on her. I had all I could do to prevent her from hurting herself."

"Dear God!"

"She accused me of somehow causing the accident, calling me a bad man. She was sure I wanted to hurt her. She had been conditioned to think of the father she barely remembered as an animal. Damn," he groaned, closing his eyes in defeat. "Since moving here I'd finally begun to hope I was reaching her. She loves the woods, especially the deer. They've never hurt her like people have," he muttered. "She tolerates my presence now, although she'll probably never be able to trust me."

"I'm sure that's not true," she murmured, shaking her head in repudiation. "If you'll just give her time . . ."

"That's all I have to give her," he sighed his defeat. "She won't accept love from me, and I've learned not to expect it. Only now . . . since your arrival, I'm beginning to hope."

"Why are you telling me all this?" she questioned. "I'm just a stranger. What will my knowing accomplish?"

His eyes seemed to sear her with the concentration of his stare. Their color had changed to a murky green-brown, and she found herself catching her breath at the brooding quality reflected in their depths. His answer to her question broke the spell being woven around them, and she expelled the air in her lungs with a choked gasp.

"Dawn seems drawn to you," he replied. "I was

shocked when I found her curled at the foot of your bed. She's always avoided strangers before this. Tonight she was genuinely concerned about you."

At his reference to the scene his daughter had interrupted, Eden flushed. She lowered her head in an attempt to avoid his eyes, flinching when his hand cupped her chin.

"Don't touch me," she muttered, backing nervously away.

"You're right," he sighed. "What happened tonight was unforgivable, but please try to understand. I'm a man with the normal urges, Eden. I know you probably think I'm some kind of depraved sex maniac, but I can assure you I acted out of character. Normally I pride myself on my control, but where you were concerned, I failed miserably."

"Just as long as you realize I dislike you as much or more than you do me, Mr. Lassiter!"

"Will your dislike stop you from trying to help my daughter?"

Eden stared at him, aghast at his assumption. She shook her head in a savagely negative gesture, glaring at him with all the pent-up dislike she could muster. How dare he think she'd let a child suffer for any reason, she thought, appalled at the depths of emotion this man was making her feel.

"You'll go to her, then?"

Without another word Eden knocked lightly on the door. "Dawn, will you let me in?"

Placing her ear against the wood, she heard a slight rustling from within. She suspected the child was standing close, but Dawn refused to answer. "All right, honey, I understand," she said, her tones conveying as much gentle confidence as she could muster. "I'll see you tomorrow," she promised. "Maybe we can be friends. I need you to be my friend, sweetheart."

"Tell her you'll be sleeping in the room you had last night."

Eden frowned at the whispered command, her own anxiety resurfacing.

"I won't stay here with you," she muttered.

"I understand," he flushed, self-disgust evident in his voice. "Please, don't be afraid of me, Eden. I can take anything but that. I promise you, I only want Dawn to know you'll be here if she changes her mind."

With trepidation, Eden looked up at him. She didn't trust him. How could she, after his earlier actions? Still, she didn't see how she could avoid complying with his wishes. There was the child to think about. If her presence in the house tonight might help her, she had no other choice.

"Dawn, I'll be sleeping in my old room tonight. Will you come and visit me again?"

No sound came from inside, not even the slight rustling she had heard earlier, and Eden's heart sank. Turning, she walked silently down the hallway in the direction of her former room. She wasn't even aware that Steven followed until he spoke from behind. Eden turned, an unconscious wariness in her eyes.

"Don't worry," he murmured, a teasing slant to his mobile mouth. "You won't have to bother locking your door. I'm not interested in frightened does."

"I'm not worried," she lied, doing her best to bolster her flagging spirits. "Good night, Mr. Lassiter."

"Good night, Miss McAllister," he taunted, his eyes derisive. Without another word he turned back in the direction they had come, long, loping strides bearing him swiftly out of sight.

Eden drew a ragged breath, relief making her feel almost faint. The events of this evening had served to make her feel even less able to cope than usual, and she didn't see how she was going to be able to bear being trapped here for another two days.

How far she'd come from the eagerness of yesterday, she mourned, tiredly preparing for bed. Everything had seemed to be working toward building her confidence in herself, but Steven Lassiter had succeeded in reducing her to her normally uncertain state of mind.

She slipped beneath the covers and pulled them over her like a shield, her inborn shyness and timid nature making her want to rage in disgust at herself. Even when being assaulted, she'd been frozen, unable to offer more than a token protest to Steven's handling of her. Her mind's eye relived every detail as she lay there, cringing at the painful memories.

Sleep was just beginning to relax her defenses when she gasped, her eyes widening in appalled discovery. With her guard lowered, thoughts she'd been unaware of surged to the surface, and she moaned aloud in repudiation. At the time, those moments in Steven's arms had been distorted by anger, but now, now that his disclosures had forced her to see him in a newer and even pitiable light, she faced the truth. If Dawn hadn't interrupted them, how long would it have been before the spiraling sensations she'd begun to feel surged out of control? From the very beginning she'd been fighting an attraction to Steven Lassiter. That's why he was able to instigate emotional reactions in her that made her a stranger to herself. Dear God, how could she ache for the touch of a bitter stranger?

Slow tears poured down her cheeks, and she muffled desperate sobs in her pillow. *John, oh, John! Why did you have to die? Why was I left behind?* There wasn't any answer to her torment, as she knew there wouldn't be. Hadn't she asked the same questions over and over again in the hospital, when they'd finally told her she'd never see her husband or child again?

A feather touch on her shoulder intruded on her self-absorption. Slowly she turned her head to see Dawn standing quietly beside the bed. Eden pulled the covers back, as her eyes begged for the comfort she knew they could give each other. Silently the child crawled in beside her, and Eden enfolded her little body in her arms. Sighing, she closed her eyes. "My little girl," she whispered, "my baby!" Neither heard the opening of the bedroom door, nor the muffled groan uttered by the man filling the doorway.

CHAPTER FOUR

Early morning dawned with murky insistence; the feeble light of the fog-laden sky penetrating Eden's tightly closed lids without mercy. Turning her head with caution toward the opposite side of the bed, she noticed the small indentation in the pillow with a sense of painful frustration. Slow tears formed, tears she couldn't allow to fall.

There had been too many tears over the years, she realized. For the first time, in too long to remember, her sleep had been free of nightmares, subconsciously comforted by the presence of the child. The child! Steven's disclosures of Dawn's background still made her flinch inwardly. How could she lie here, pitying herself, when that little girl's pain went so much deeper?

Her own loss had been sharp and incisive, cutting into the fabric of her life with tragic force. But Dawn . . . her torture had been a prolonged agony so great she was still staggering beneath its weight. In effect she had lost not only her mother, because good or bad Elaine had been the only mother the child could lay claim to, but she had lost her father as well.

If something wasn't done, and soon, to pull the child from the realms of nightmare imaginings, Eden felt she

57

would never escape. Evidently Steven, as much as he loved his daughter, hadn't been able to find the key to unlock Dawn's mind. After three years it was doubtful if such a monumental task would ever be accomplished. Steven had likened Dawn to her mother, Eden remembered. Was it true? Was there some kind of inherited instability running through the veins of such a small, defenseless little girl?

Eden frowned, getting out of bed with sluggish movements. She noticed her suitcase standing just inside the bathroom door; its significance caused a slow-burning tide to color her cheeks. Steven must have gone for it in the night, but she found she couldn't be appreciative of the courtesy. The thought of his entering her room, seeing his daughter sleeping beside her, filled her with a strange uneasiness.

Her bath was quick and functional. She intended to soak away some of her tension in the gold ceramic tub, but she found herself incapable of relaxation. She felt cut off, isolated, and quite unable to bear the idea of facing Steven again after the traumatic happenings of last night. Somehow the suspicion that he had been in her room and watched her sleep made her feel vulnerable.

Had he guessed how close he had been to gaining a response from her? As she dressed in a plain white blouse and navy slacks, her thoughts caused her fingers to fumble with the fastening at her waist. To her shame, she couldn't seem to stop remembering how his hard, masculine fingertips had aroused her into tingling, vibrant need.

Biting down on the fullness of her lower lip didn't do much to distract her thoughts, and she walked to the door with brittle determination. She opened it slowly, needing all of her willpower to make herself leave the dubious safety of the bedroom. She was puzzled by the silence that seemed to spread sinuously around her from the vastness of the rooms. Her footsteps echoed hollowly on the hardwood floors of the hall and dining room. Bracing herself to enter the kitchen, she was relieved when Mrs. Adams bustled through the swinging door.

"Well, dear, are you ready for your breakfast?"

"I—I'm really not very hungry, Mrs. Adams," Eden replied nervously, trying to peer into the other room through the still-swinging door.

"Are you looking for Mr. Lassiter?"

"W-what? Oh, no, I . . ." Eden stammered, looking anywhere but at the coyly smiling woman.

"Now, that's all right," Mrs. Adams reassured her with bracing insistence, clearly not believing her. "I know how it is, dear. I can remember the days when just the sight of my Joe set shivers to running up my spine."

"Oh, Mrs. Adams," Eden gasped. "You don't understand. Mr. Lassiter and I aren't . . . well, we're not . . ."

"Don't you go thinking you owe me any explanations," Mrs. Adams interrupted. "I can put two and two together as well as anyone, not that it takes much sense to tell which way the wind's blowing. Why, you're the first female other than myself and little Dawn who's been in this house since the building of it. It's as plain as the nose on your face what's happening between yourself and Mr. Steven!"

Eden wanted to scream a repudiation, but couldn't bear the thought of hurting Mrs. Adams's feelings. It would take more courage than she possessed to enter into an explanation. Even the thought of the embarrassment it would entail filled her with anguish. Visions of herself and Steven locked together in each other's arms entered the forefront of her mind, and she gasped at the evocativeness of the sensual memory.

"Mrs. Adams, I'm here on business!" Even as she uttered the reason for her presence in the house, she could tell by the beaming grin on the older woman's face that her words weren't getting through.

"Oh, I know you're here to work on the building of that lovely resort Mr. Steven's planning."

Relief surged through Eden. At last she was getting somewhere in erasing the impression of herself and Steven Lassiter as a cozy twosome in Mrs. Adams's mind. The effort had seemed almost greater than she could handle, she thought, a bubble of half-hysterical laughter threatening to escape from between her quivering lips.

"Thank God you understand," Eden gasped, a small smile replacing the tense trembling of her lips.

"What does Mary understand, darling?"

At the sound of his voice beside her, Eden turned, her face whitening with shock. Taking advantage of her silence, Steven locked his arms around her waist, pulling her still and unresisting body against the hardness of his. His eyes looked almost green now, Eden thought inconsequentially, just before his head lowered to block out the sight. Her tiny gasp was muffled by the warm insistence of his mouth, and in Eden's shocked state Mrs. Adams's approving chuckle sounded almost unbearably loud.

"What-what do you think you're doing?" she gasped, finally regaining the use of her limbs and pulling away from his warmth.

"Come into the study," he commanded peremptorily, sending a warning glance in the direction of the kitchen, through which Mrs. Adams had just disappeared.

"I'm not going anywhere with you," she snapped, wiping the back of her hand childishly over her mouth in an attempt to erase the feel of his lips against hers.

Without further discussion, he reached out and grasped Eden's wrist, pulling her in the direction of the study. *This is getting to be a habit,* she thought, not finding the idea particularly amusing. As soon as they reached the study, she attempted to exit through the welcome haven of the open French doors across the room, but Steven stopped her flight with little effort.

Furious with his manhandling, Eden placed all the force she could muster behind her swinging arm, and a slap resounded sickeningly in the quietness of the room.

"Damn you," he snapped, taking her shoulders in his hands and administering shaking retribution. "Will you just give me a chance to explain, you little shrew!"

"I don't know what possessed you," she raged.

"Look, Mary was preparing one of the guest rooms near you for a friend of mine, and she saw me leaving your room this morning. She's the biggest gossip in the neighborhood," he rasped. "Did you want her to think you're my mistress?"

"What difference does it make? I'll be gone by Monday, anyway, and I don't think the sullying of my good name will spread all the way to Los Angeles, do you?"

Apparently deciding to overlook the taunting insolence in her voice, Steven released her and moved in the direction of his desk. Seating himself on the edge in the same languid pose she remembered so vividly from the day before, he crossed his arms over his chest. Eden tried to ignore the way the movement caused his forearms to bulge, or the way the green silk of the shirt he wore clung lovingly to his shoulders. She didn't want to acknowledge the reason for her suddenly dry mouth either.

"Are you sure you'll be going home?"

At the question, Eden paused, confusion straining her features. "Of course," she whispered, moistening her lips with the tip of her tongue until she noticed his chameleon eyes following the movement.

A confident smile creased the corners of his mouth. Eden watched the shaking of his head with a staggering sense of inevitability. Somehow she knew his next words would trap her inexorably in a situation not of her choosing, but she couldn't seem to do anything to stop him.

"I thought it was your burning ambition to be here to supervise the building of the resort," Steven stated.

"Y-you made it clear that I wasn't suitable for the job," she stammered.

"And if I've changed my mind?"

Eden felt the sickening impact of his words cutting off her breath. Gasping, she stared at him, her eyes brown pools of misery. "What are you saying?" she murmured, her voice an infinitesimal thread of sound.

"I'm offering you the chance to do the work you came for," he said, getting abruptly to his feet. He uncrossed his arms, instead bracing his palms on his hips. "Well, what's your answer?"

Eden couldn't accept without knowing the reasons for the reversal of his decision. She didn't want him to think he was buying more than her professional services as an architect. Before she lost her nerve, she would question him, but she found it hard going when she met the sudden derision in his eyes.

"Don't worry, it's not your body I'm after," he retorted. "When I delivered your luggage this morning, Dawn woke up. She smiled at me," he whispered, "actually smiled. I don't know what it is about you that seems to be reaching her, but I'd be foolish not to follow up on it. You want the job. I want help for my daughter. Is it a fair enough exchange?"

"I would stay and help if I could," she said, feeling tormented with indecision. Helpless, she wrung her hands together, turning to stare through the opening in the French doors. "What about the gossip my presence would create?" she snapped.

"There'd be no gossip if everyone took it for granted we were engaged," he replied, the silkiness of his voice flowing over her until she shivered with reaction. Moving away from the draft emanating from the open door, it was her turn to cross her arms around herself.

"That's why you staged that scene for Mrs. Adams?"

"Of course," he replied. "Why else?"

"Oh, it's impossible," she cried, once more turning to face him. "Surely we don't have to resort to that kind of a farce? I'll be working on the project as an architect. Surely people wouldn't assume that we're . . . we're . . ."

"Lovers?" he rasped, moving across the room until he stood directly in front of her. "Why wouldn't they?"

"Because I—I'm not exactly the picture of seduction," she cried, goaded beyond endurance by his taunt.

To her surprise and mortification he grasped her chin, raising her head and studying her eyes with an intensity that shook her to the soles of her sneaker-shod feet. She attempted to pull away, but again she experienced a weakening sensation in her body from the warmth of his fingers against her skin. What was the hold this man had over her?

His gaze seemed to be burning through her, and her

pupils dilated in unwilling arousal as his head lowered slowly toward hers.

"Soft little doe eyes," he murmured gently, his tone almost absentminded. "Don't you know what eyes like yours can do to a man?"

Eden was fascinated by the seductive movements of his mouth, her bemusement blinding her to everything around her. She found herself holding her breath, not wanting to do or say anything to break the enchantment surrounding her. Sensing her need, a small smile curved his lips as they moved closer, and she almost gasped as their warm breaths mingled together.

In a daydream she felt his flesh against hers, their mouths twisting, merging, while seeking for ways to prolong their pleasure.

Her thoughts whirled in confusion. Even with John she'd never felt this fierce physical attraction. Oh, she supposed they'd been happy enough, but they hadn't reached the passionate heights she suspected she could find with this man. Their lives had been filled with contentment and the love they had shared for the small daughter they'd been blessed with.

Now there was only John to care for Shelley. As the thought reached her through blind mists of passion, she twisted out of Steven's embrace, surprised when he offered no resistance. Turning, she crossed her arms in front of her. Both John and Shelley were together in a place she couldn't reach, while she had been forced to carry on alone. She thought of Dawn—Dawn of the large blue eyes and corn-gold hair.

Eden knew very well what Dawn saw in her eyes. She was drawn toward Eden's loneliness, her agony of spirit. Dawn wasn't Shelley, but Eden had sensed from the very first that she could fill the nagging emptiness left by Shelley's death, simply by loving this child who needed her. But, dear God, how would she be able to bear losing her when the time came to leave? She couldn't . . .

She found herself violently shaking her head, rejection in every line of her stiffening body.

"Dear God, woman," Steven muttered, reaching out to clasp her shoulders. "Isn't there an ounce of pity in you?"

"You can't ask this of me," she sobbed, raising her ravaged features to his condemning gaze. Without conscious volition, words of pain and anguished loss began pouring from her, and slowly his look of condemnation changed. She didn't struggle when he cupped the back of her head to draw her face against the solid depths of his chest. Like a child, she needed to be held, and as if he sensed this, his arms tightened around her. For long moments they stood there, their earlier fires banked into comforting warmth until, with an embarrassed murmur, Eden drew away.

"I'm sorry, I didn't know," he rasped, raking shaking fingers through his burnished hair. "You're really *Mrs.* McAllister, then. Why didn't you correct me earlier?"

Eden walked toward the chair beside his desk, lowering her limp body into the security it represented for her shaking legs. "Why all the fuss over a name?" she questioned tiredly. "It just didn't seem important enough to make an issue out of whether I was a Miss or Mrs. If you like, you can make it Ms."

"You're right. We're hardly close enough friends for explanations to be necessary between us," he remarked, handing her a large, snowy handkerchief without further comment.

Eden took it gratefully. She must look an absolute mess,

65

she thought. What had possessed her to give way like that? As soon as the thought teased the confusion clouding her brain, she knew the answer. Since her arrival she had been beset by such a barrage of conflicting emotions she found herself totally out of control. She had worked so hard to build up her life, she thought. Now, in a short space of time, this man and his child had lifted the veils enveloping her independence. They had shown her needs within herself which had been severely suppressed for too long.

"I'll arrange your flight home as soon as it's possible," Steven continued, interrupting her thoughts. He moved to look outside through the French doors in almost the identical posture she herself had used such a short time ago. Staring at the broad back, Eden wondered if he, too, used the beauty of the outdoors as a solace for bruised and aching feelings.

As if to confirm her thought, he shook his head violently. His clenched fist slammed into the wall, causing the glass panes to rattle alarmingly. "God, fate can certainly play some monstrous tricks!"

His words opened floodgates in Eden's mind, and the blood pounded in her ears. Twisting the handkerchief in shaking hands she stared down at the white square of fabric, her thoughts chaotic. From the moment she had set foot on Lassiter property, fate had begun spreading silken tendrils around her, but she would escape. She would! A sickness pervaded her tense stomach muscles, a prelude to the wrenching anguish she would have to face if she allowed herself to become any more entwined with the lives of these people.

Once back in Los Angeles she would force herself to push Steven Lassiter and Dawn into the background of her life. Her work would be a solace, one she'd used effectively six years ago, and after a while the memories of this embittered man and his little girl would cease to haunt her.

She didn't even notice when Steven left the room. The closing of the door was the first indication she had to tell her that once again she was alone. Her head felt heavy when she lifted it to look around her in bewildered surprise, her neck feeling almost too fragile to bear its weight. As she studied her surroundings, Eden felt strange, as if everything should have changed within the last half hour. Of course, nothing had. The bookcases ranging the far wall from floor to ceiling were still in place. The cold, gutted cavern of the fireplace was still enclosed by the myriad colored rocks. No! If there'd been any change, it had taken place within herself, and the fanciful idea was frightening.

With a muffled moan she jumped to her feet, feeling a claustrophobic need to escape. She hurried through the French doors as if the hounds of hell were at her heels. She didn't know or care where she was going, intent only on finding consolation.

Eden's flight stopped abruptly on the edge of a little clearing. Dropping to her knees, her breath coming from her chest in painful spurts, she sat hidden from the clearing by a dense clump of red and green manzanita bushes. For long moments she sat huddled, her head lowered to rest upon her drawn-up knees. The dampness of the ground slowly filtered through her slacks, and she wrapped her arms tighter around her legs in an attempt to stop the shivers coursing through her body.

She knew it was foolish, sitting like a child unaware of its well-being, but she didn't care. The smell of crushed grass rose to her nostrils, mingling with the scents of trees and earth and the heavily musty odor of the fog-laden air. Slowly her breath returned to normal, the last of her tension a shuddering sigh borne away by a gentle breeze.

Eden didn't know what alerted her to the fact she was no longer alone. She wasn't conscious of the crackling of a twig or even the brush of clothing indicating another presence. There was only one person who moved with such fey grace, and her head moved upward slowly.

"Hello, Dawn!"

"You're in my secret place," she murmured, a wary look pinching the small features together in a scowl.

Eden decided that possibly the only way to reach this hostile child was by an adult approach, and she took a deep, steadying breath.

"I'm sorry," she apologized. "Would you like me to leave?"

A look of consternation crossed Dawn's face. "No," she muttered grudgingly. "I guess you can stay for a while."

Eden smiled her thanks, leaning back with her palms supporting her weight. For long moments the tableau was unbroken, with herself apparently enjoying the quiet solace of the little glade, and Dawn poised as if ready for flight should the necessity arise. Eden's patience was finally rewarded when Dawn lowered herself to sit beside her.

"Why did you come here?"

At the child's question Eden shrugged her shoulders, a wry grimace curving her mouth. "I was running away, I suppose."

"From my daddy?" Dawn's question was accompanied with a strangely adult nod. "I do that sometimes, when I'm afraid," she admitted.

"But why should you be afraid of your daddy, honey? He loves you very much."

"He doesn't. He doesn't love me," she cried, beginning to edge slightly farther away from Eden.

Eden decided a change of subject was called for and quickly. "Well, I didn't run away from your father. He's been very nice to me," she lied. "I—I was running away from a big hurt in here," she explained, touching her breast, watching Dawn's face intently as she did so. "You see, honey, sometimes memories aren't very pleasant, and even after we're safe, they can hurt terribly."

"Who hurt you? W-was it your mommy?"

Dawn's voice was a mere thread of sound, and Eden closed her eyes against the pity welling up inside of her for this bewildered little girl. *At least I can understand the source of my hurt,* she thought. How much worse it would be to bear pain, and not completely remember or understand its source.

"Dawn, I know your mommy hurt you, but she didn't mean to," Eden replied, praying silently for the right words to reach the child sitting so rigidly beside her. "Sometimes people love you and still do things to hurt you. That's what happened to me. My husband loved me, but he drove our car much too fast. There was a storm, and I was trying to comfort my little girl. The car crashed, and when I woke up in the hospital, I'd been hurt. But my husband hadn't wanted me to be. Do you understand?"

"Where's your little girl? Did you leave her with strange people?"

"No!" Eden whispered, her face twisting with pain. "My little girl and her daddy are in heaven, Dawn."

She pressed her lips together tightly to prevent their trembling. She hadn't wanted to upset Dawn. She had only been trying to show the child she wasn't alone in her grief, and now she had probably made matters worse.

69

What had possessed her? She raged silently. Was she trying to comfort the child, or herself?

"My mommy went there too," Dawn nodded. "I ... sometimes I miss her. Do-do you miss your little girl?"

Eden nodded, not trusting her voice for a moment. After a while she murmured, "Very much."

A small hand gripped hers, and Dawn edged closer to Eden's side. Afraid to make any movement, Eden remained locked in stillness, until she felt the brush of a small head against her shoulder.

"I'll be your little girl," she promised. "Then you won't be lonesome anymore."

"I—I'd like that more than anything," she gasped, reaching out with her other arm to enfold the child in the warmth of her clasp. Slow tears trickled down Eden's cheeks, becoming lost within the downy softness of Dawn's hair.

"What's your name?" Dawn's words were muffled against her breast, but Eden heard them.

"Eden," she replied. "You know, like in the Garden of Eden."

She was rewarded by a low chuckle. "I like that name," Dawn sighed. "You smell nice, like a garden."

"Thank you," Eden laughed, brushing the child's hair back with trembling fingers. "You smell nice too. Like a little girl."

"Oh, Eden, they're coming," Dawn whispered, pointing toward the clearing. "Look!"

Following the direction of Dawn's pointing finger, Eden looked, and drew her breath in sharply. A small brown deer was entering the clearing, and for the first time Eden noticed a mound in its center. She couldn't make it out, but apparently the animal knew what it was, because she was obviously moving in that direction.

"What's wrong with her, Dawn?" Eden had noticed the way the animal was dragging her back legs behind her.

"I think she was runned over," the child replied. "I feed her so she won't die."

The animal sniffed the air, her head moving from side to side as if checking for danger. Apparently satisfied, she struck the earth with her forepaw, and a tiny spotted fawn moved toward its mother from a concealed place in the trees. Together they moved toward the center of the clearing, the little fawn cavorting playfully while its mother lowered her head to eat Dawn's offerings.

"Thank you for letting me stay in your secret place." Eden sighed, getting to her feet after the animals once more gained the shelter of the woods. "They were beautiful, your little friends."

As they turned to walk back in the direction of the house, Dawn slowly tucked her hand within Eden's. Looking down at the child's bent head, she felt shaken by her feelings.

"You can come with me to feed them lots of times," Dawn promised. Although her tone was apparently indifferent, Eden felt Dawn's hand tighten around hers. With a lump forming achingly within her throat, Eden knew without a doubt that her fate had been sealed by what had just happened. Now, no matter what it cost her, she knew she couldn't leave!

CHAPTER FIVE

Eden blew an errant strand of hair from her face with pursed lips. She was concentrating on the blueprints spread across Steven's desk, and didn't notice the grin creasing the mouth of the man by her side until a teasing hand flipped the curl irritatingly downward once more.

"For heaven's sake, James," she protested. "Can't you be serious for more than five minutes at a time?"

" 'There was a little girl, who had a little curl, right in the middle of her forehead,' " he chanted, shaking his head at the exasperation crossing Eden's features.

"I know," she grimaced, a hand pressing the ache in the small of her back as she straightened from her crouched position. " 'And when she was good, she was very, very good, and when she was bad, she was horrid.' You see, I remember my nursery rhymes as well as the next person."

"Hmmm, can you be horrid, sweet Eden?" he murmured, his voice a sexy drawl which belied the creases slanting his twinkling blue eyes. "Now I'm finally making progress!"

"If you're not careful, I'm going to write that girl of yours and tell her what a lecherous old man you are," she threatened, her own smile answering his.

" 'Gather ye rosebuds while ye may,' " he quipped, his

deceptive little-boy face sobering into injured reproach. "I just can't understand why you won't let me play in your garden, love of my life!"

Eden burst into a peal of delighted laughter, the clear, bell-like tones reverberating against the study walls. James Mills was the head of the Sacramento construction firm of Expansion Unlimited who had contracted to handle the building of Steven's resort. He was Steven's friend, which was why he was staying in the house, but over the last two months he and Eden had developed a warm friendship. Since a great amount of her time was spent working with the tall, thin man beside her, she felt she'd known him forever.

"James, you're a fool!"

"No," he sighed, a quirk tilting one sandy brow. "I'm only a fool where you're concerned, Eden. Lust is wreaking havoc with my life."

"Am I interrupting?"

Eden gasped and whirled around, nervously putting slightly more distance between herself and James. "No, of course not, S-Steven," she stammered, all of the earlier animation leaving her face.

Apparently James couldn't sense the tension springing to life in the room with Steven's entrance, because to Eden's consternation he placed a lazy arm around her waist, drawing her to his side.

"Steve, you've certainly found a winner in this girl," he grinned. "If you're not careful, I'm going to take her away from you!"

She could sense James's head turning in her direction when he spoke the damning words, and knew he didn't see the fleeting savagery on the face of the man blocking the doorway. Eden saw, and swallowed with difficulty.

74

Really! she thought. What right did he have looking at her with such contempt? She had fulfilled her part of their bargain, so he had absolutely nothing to complain about. Even agreeing to go on with their farce of an engagement had been achieved with as little fuss as possible on her part, convinced for Dawn's sake of the necessity for the subterfuge.

Although their mock-engagement rankled Eden, she did her best to pretend it didn't bother her to live a lie. Still, she couldn't help blaming Steven for the nerve-wracking uncertainty of her position in his household. James's arrival, and the fact that they worked well together, should have relieved the pressure she was under, but it hadn't. Quite the contrary! Although she knew that Steven and James were old friends, one certainly couldn't prove it by Steven's attitude over the last couple of months. At times he seemed almost unbearably irritated by James's ready laughter and clowning demeanor.

Even now the tension emanating from Steven was marked, and she was at a loss to understand his attitude. Studying the features of each man in turn, she absently noticed the differences between them. Where Steven's personality was introspective and serious, James's reflected infallible good humor and a light, breezy attitude to life. That was why she was comfortable in his presence, she realized. He made her forget her own seriousness, however briefly, the way a rascally but beloved brother might. With Steven it was different! When he looked at her with brooding eyes, something inside her met and joined the inner pain she sensed eating at him, until her whole body became clumsy with tense nervousness.

"James, you *are* a fool!" Steven's laughter was harsh,

but apparently James didn't notice, because he grinned widely in Steven's direction.

"Ouch, buddy," he grimaced, his eyes dancing. "You never used to be so possessive with your women. Why, I remember a little redhead you positively begged me to . . ."

"Take off my hands?" Steven's eyes sliced meaningfully in Eden's direction. Without making an issue out of it, he brushed James's hand from her waist and drew her instead into the circle of his own arm. Over her head he said, "I've mellowed since those days, my friend. Now I keep my women to myself."

Eden stiffened with resentment. "Look, if you two are through discussing your boyhood memories, I'd like to walk down to the bus stop to pick up Dawn."

As if the mention of his daughter were enough to distract him from his conversation with James, Steven released her. "How's she doing in school?"

"Wonderfully," she replied, forgetting her earlier resentment long enough to smile up at him.

"She's a smart little monkey," James laughed. "Has she been having trouble in class?"

She knew James was aware of the bare outlines of the difficulty Steven had had with his late wife, because she had been there herself when Steven explained to James Dawn's particularly obnoxious behavior one evening, soon after he had arrived. Still, she didn't feel it was her place to answer, and she sent a meaningful glance in Steven's direction.

He complied, but Eden sensed it was done grudgingly by the impatient brevity of his explanation.

"Poor little kid," James sighed, shaking his head. "Yet she's beginning to come out of it," he encouraged, smiling at Eden. "In the short time I've been here, she's like two different children."

"Oh, yes," Eden smiled. "The teacher says she'd never have believed anyone could change so much in such a short space of time. Although she always did as she was told, she never mingled with the other children, or spoke other than when absolutely necessary. Now she's even volunteering to answer questions, and the other day she began talking about another little girl in her class. I don't think she knows how to go about making friends, but I think a packet of 'Hello, Kitty' stickers might help."

"Hello what?" Steven's brow furrowed in puzzled inquiry, and Eden laughed.

" 'Hello, Kitty' stickers," she explained, her brown eyes dancing. "Don't you know anything?"

"Apparently not," he grumbled, leaning against the desk. "Just what are you talking about?"

"There's a store that carries a line of objects geared to appeal to children," she explained. "All the kids have them, according to Dawn. I gather they trade with each other during recess. I promised Dawn I'd take her into Redding after school today!" Eden's eager words faltered on seeing Steven frown. "I—I know I should have asked your permission first, but I was so excited, I just didn't think. This is the first time Dawn's shown any interest in the things that appeal to a child of her age."

Steven saw James's puzzled frown swivel in Eden's direction at the note of nervous apology in her voice, and he had to keep himself from swearing in frustration. With commendable calm he said, "You know you don't have to ask my permission to take Dawn anywhere, Eden. My God, if it weren't for you, she'd still be wandering the woods, feeding that wounded deer she identifies with!"

"What deer?" James asked.

Biting her lip in indecision, Eden avoided Steven's eyes by turning to James. "Apparently the poor animal was hit by a car. She drags her lower body around helplessly, attempting to forage for her small fawn. Dawn sets food in a clearing and hides behind the bushes while they eat. Sometimes"—she smiled eagerly, warming to her story—"they let us . . ."

"Eden, have you been encouraging her in this nonsense?"

This time there was no masking Steven's anger as he raked Eden with a basilisk stare.

"Whoops. Sorry to rush off, folks," James murmured, rolling up the blueprints in a haphazard fashion and making for the door. "I just remembered something on the site I'd better check."

Eden glared furiously in the direction of his departing back. *Fine friend he is!* she thought. Avoiding Steven's eyes, she attempted to restore order to the chaos his desk had become. She could feel his gaze boring into her back through the buttercup-yellow sundress she wore, and she shivered, wishing she had donned the matching jacket. With her arms bare, she felt somehow more vulnerable.

"Eden, I can tell by your avoidance of the subject that I've hit a sore spot," he muttered furiously. "You might as well face me and get it over with!"

Taking a deep breath, Eden turned, levering herself on the top of his desk and crossing her white-sandaled feet together at the ankles.

"Don't think that little-girl pose is going to help matters," he muttered. "In that dress I don't see you as much of a child."

Raising her head in defiance, Eden once again felt that

78

strange awareness between them, an awareness she didn't consciously try to create. Since that night so long ago she'd done everything she could to avoid being alone with him, and now, because of the mention of Dawn's deer, she found herself in the kind of situation she tried to avoid.

If she had any sense, she would have kept her explanation for James until they were alone. It wasn't as if she hadn't known how Steven felt. When she'd first told him about going with Dawn to feed the animals, he had demanded she try to discourage his daughter from such an undertaking, she remembered.

"I meant to discourage Dawn," she muttered, staring down at her hands. "Only somehow . . . I couldn't do it. I know the deer doesn't need help finding food now that everything's plentiful. But when winter comes, foraging will be much more difficult for a wounded animal. The important thing is that Dawn feels like she's helping. Can't you understand that?"

"Yes, but what happens when the animal doesn't show up someday? The deer will die anyway, Eden, and there's nothing you or Dawn can do to prevent it," he retorted, shaking his head in repudiation. "She's half dead now, and if I had any sense, I'd put her out of her misery!"

Eden jumped to her feet, her shocked eyes holding his for endless moments. "You couldn't do anything so cruel," she gasped.

"Sometimes one has to be cruel to be kind."

"Steven, please," she whispered, her body trembling with the force of the slow fear building within her. "This isn't the time for clichés. It's taken so long for me to reach Dawn, to teach her to see you as a father and not some kind of monster. If you hurt that animal, she would never forgive you!"

Steven walked toward her, a shuttered expression on his face. Silently he reached out for her shoulders, bare under the thin straps of her dress. She fought to control her pounding pulses at the touch of his hands against the softness of her tanned skin. She thought she'd succeeded until she noticed his eyes dwelling intently on the throbbing pulse point in her throat.

"And you," he whispered, searching her eyes intently. "How do you see me, Eden?"

Eden felt flustered, unable to answer while looking into the warmth of his eyes. Her own eyes fell until she found herself staring in fascination at the muscular brown column of his throat, her gaze becoming riveted on the patch of chest hair peeping from the deepened V of his shirt. The sight weakened her composure still further, and she edgily tried to back away from the clasp of his hands. His grip tightened and she felt herself being pressed against the well-developed length of his powerful body.

"Steven, I . . ."

"Why do you flinch whenever I get near you?" he demanded, one hand sliding up her arm, lingering on the soft skin of her shoulder as if eager to imprint her on his sensitive palm. "Do you see me as some kind of monster, the way my daughter used to? You're a woman," he muttered, leaning forward until he inhaled the aroma of her hair, "not a child indulging in youthful fantasies. A woman with warmth, and well able to respond to a man's desires, even though you try to hide it. I know I've acted the brute with you, baby, but I can be gentle. Let me show you. . . ."

True to his promise, he was gentle, his mouth capturing hers with mind-shattering finesse. His lips moved in a slow, brushing motion across hers, stopping now and then to allow his tongue to coax apart the trembling flesh she kept closed to him.

Eden couldn't tolerate the sensations he was arousing. Jerking her head aside, she gasped for breath, all the while trying to place distance between them. With a sigh, Steven released her, an impatient scowl darkening his features. His frown didn't do much to bolster her sagging courage. She wanted to erase that glare of displeasure from his brow, and she had to fight herself to keep from willingly returning to his arms. Trying to keep her mind resolutely turned toward escaping, she muttered, "Steven, please. James . . ."

"Ah, yes," he muttered, his fingers becoming punishing bands preventing her retreat. "What about dear old James?"

Her brow creasing in a puzzled frown, she stared into the glittering depths of his eyes, disturbed by the darkening shadows building there. "N-nothing, only he might walk in at any moment."

"And that would bother you?"

"Of course! I wouldn't relish being caught . . ."

"In the arms of your fiancé? Is that what you're trying to say?"

"Why are you trying to twist my words, Steven? Are you looking for a quarrel? If something's bothering you, then for heaven's sake tell me. I don't like being used as a whipping boy!"

To Eden's dismay, she watched the color drain from Steven's face, a white rim of furiously suppressed emotion encircling his compressed lips. She didn't understand what she had said to bring about such a transformation, but she wasn't long left in doubt. His hand lifted to cup her chin, and with incredulous surprise she noticed his fingers were trembling.

"Every time I come near you, you jump like a scalded cat, and yet when James enters a room, you light up like a Christmas tree. Don't you think I've noticed you whispering together in corners, stopping as soon as I walk into the room? I'm sick to death of the sound of your laughter, the way your eyes sparkle whenever he gets within three feet of you."

"You don't understand," she protested, laying a placating hand on his arm. "James and I are friends, and we enjoy each other's company. We haven't deliberately left you out, it's just that sometimes you aren't exactly what I would call approachable, Steven."

"Are you telling me that if I were more . . . approachable, that you and I could be friends?"

His thumb was moving slowly along the fluid lines of her throat, sending confused signals through her bloodstream.

"I . . . I . . ."

"You know I want more than friendship from you, don't you?" he whispered, his mouth lowering to within inches of hers. "Well, don't let good buddy James fool you, sweetheart. Given the opportunity, he'll take what you're offering with as much alacrity as I would!"

His words hit her with the force of a blow. How dare he suggest that she was making a play for James! He was taking an innocent relationship and trying to make it appear sordid and cheap, but he wasn't going to get away with it. Not by a long shot!

"James understands our relationship as well as I do," she snapped, jerking her chin from his grasp. "It's you who refuses to face facts, Steven. To James, flirting with the nearest woman is as natural as drawing breath, and I'd be a fool to take him seriously. I play along, but I do not, I repeat, *do not* offer myself to any man, for any reason!"

Eden kept her head levelled at his chest, desperately concentrating on the swirling pattern of his silk shirt. The silence built around them until she wanted to scream, and when he spoke again, she almost gave in to the impulse.

"Would you offer yourself to a man who was slowly going out of his mind with wanting you?" He paused, his fingers gently tracing the fine bones of her shoulder with maddening slowness, his eyes following the movement compulsively. "Since James arrived, my life has been hell, watching you smile at him, hearing your laughter. I want your warmth, honey, and I'll see James in hell beside me before I'll let him have you. As far as James is concerned, you're my fiancée, and that places boundaries he'd better not attempt to step over where you're concerned."

With self-disgust, Eden could feel herself mentally backing away from this confrontation. He wanted her, and she just wasn't ready to face admitting the change this would make in their relationship. For too long she had held herself aloof, afraid of the quiet strength she could feel in him. If their engagement had its basis in reality, she would bask in that strength, but as it was, the power that emanated from him depleted her own reserves, weakening her will until she barely recognized herself.

"P-please, I . . . I'll be late picking up Dawn." As soon as the words spilled from her shaking mouth, she could have kicked herself. Why did she always end up in foolish confusion whenever he spoke to her? she mourned.

"When will you stop using Dawn to hide behind, Eden?"

"I—I don't know what you mean," she lied, her eyes scanning the room's isolation nervously.

"You know very well what I mean," he sighed, shaking his head in annoyance. "But you're right. This isn't the time or the place. We'll finish our discussion later, when you're not in such a *hurry.*"

He means when I'm not such a coward, she admitted honestly. As if to emphasize just how cowardly she actually was, he released her, and as she placed a welcome distance between them, she felt almost sick with relief.

Her mouth curving in a caricature of a smile, she mumbled, "I'm afraid there won't be time this evening. I thought Dawn might like to see a movie and have pizza. before coming home. I'm taking her to the new mall in Redding, the one with the enclosed theater, and it seems a shame not to make the most of her outing."

Steven moved toward the chair behind his desk. Seating himself, he leaned back, his elbows resting on the black leather upholstery. Making an arch with his hands, he observed Eden's flushed features silently over the tips of his fingers.

"You're adept at hiding, at twisting any conversations between us until you've formed a comfortable barrier, but rest assured, Eden," he murmured, his eyes beginning to lighten with amused indulgence, "there will come a time, and soon, when escape will be the last thing you want."

"Why should your fantasies have anything to do with me?"

"Don't push me, honey," he laughed, his hands moving slowly against his legs, as if his fingers sought softer, more pliable flesh. "You might get more than you bargained for!"

Watching his hands, she shivered, meeting the awareness in his gaze with the seeds of rebellion. It wasn't fair! She was doing her best to keep their relationship on an even keel, but he seemed determined to cling to the electric sensuality that leaped between them, thwarting her efforts at every turn.

With uncharacteristic determination she walked toward him, leaning forward until her palms made contact with the smooth wood of his desk.

"What are you threatening me with, Steven? Are you going to send me home? That's what you originally wanted. Well, isn't it?"

A slow tide of furious color darkened his cheeks, and she backed away from him, already beginning a stammered apology which was stopped by the shocking sound of his fist hitting the surface of the desk.

"Do you really think, after backing down earlier, that you're ready to hear about my wants?" As he spoke, he rose slowly to his feet, intimidating her with sheer masculine size.

"N-no, I just thought . . ."

"That's your trouble, Eden. You think too much," he snapped, walking over to stare out into the garden. "Oh, for God's sake, get out of here. Have a good time playing with my daughter!"

His words were a dismissal, and Eden stiffened with resentment. One moment he was holding her, whispering sweet nothings in her ear, and the next he was ordering her from his presence as if she were the lowest slave in existence! "Isn't that what I'm here for?" she retorted, turning furiously and heading for the door.

His muttered "God only—" was cut off, the rest of the sentence drowned out by the slamming of the door.

Needing to make up the time lost in fencing with the

unreasonable man she had just left, Eden decided to drive down to the bus stop. The garage was more in the mode of a carriage house, set back among the trees, and by the time she had reached it, she had managed to walk off a good portion of her anger.

Taking calming breaths, she reversed the little blue Fiat Special out into the curving drive. Although Steven had placed the car at her disposal, she avoided using it except when absolutely necessary. She didn't want any favors from Steven Lassiter. That kind of attitude didn't help their situation any, but she felt she had no alternative. She sensed, deep inside herself, how much he could hurt her if she was stupid enough to let him, and she wasn't about to lower her guard. For some inexplicable reason she knew there could be no middle ground between them, and clinging to her shield of animosity was a lot easier than allowing herself to . . .

Eden was tremendously thankful when she saw Dawn trudging up the hill toward her. She didn't want to continue her train of thought, and what better distraction than the little girl she loved so much?

"Hello, darling," she smiled through the open window of the car. "Did you think I'd forgotten my promise?"

"Are we going now?" Dawn squeaked, her body tensing in anticipation.

"Yes. Run over and hop in," Eden laughed, delighted by the eager sparkle in the child's eyes. *This is the way Dawn should always look,* she thought, her eyes following the child as she ran around the front of the car. Seldom now did she see the haunting shadows in Dawn's luminous blue eyes, and she had even begun putting on a little more weight recently, Eden mused, studying the slight tightness in the blue jumper Dawn was wearing, an exciting idea taking shape in her mind.

A secretive smile curved her mouth as Eden began the drive into Redding. Dawn, ever-sensitive to her emotions, turned in the seat, an answering smile on her face.

"Are you excited about the 'Hello, Kitty' stickers too, Eden?"

"Well, not exactly," Eden murmured, negotiating the turn which would take them into town. "What do you think about buying some new clothes? Would you like that?"

"Could I get a skirt with a little jacket like Mary Ann has?"

"I don't see why not, if that's what you'd like," she said, her smile deepening at the breathless note in Dawn's voice.

"And maybe some jeans with little squiggles on the back pockets?" she questioned hopefully.

"Does Mary Ann have those too?"

Dawn nodded, her eyes round with excitement.

"Then jeans with squiggles it is," she laughed, stopping by the bank briefly before hurrying on to the lot of the gray-fronted mall.

Later, snuggling in the warmth of her bed, Eden reviewed the evening with satisfaction. They had watched a Disney film, exiting the theater to search for a shop catering to preteens. The highlight of the outing, as far as she was concerned, had been when Dawn stopped outside a shop called Tobacco 'n' Brew. Lovely smells filtered past the open frontage, and Eden sniffed the mingled odors of sweet tobacco and freshly ground coffee pleasurably.

"Dawn, I don't think we'll find your stickers in this

shop," she laughed, her eyes scanning the mainly masculine accoutrements of the well-stocked shelves.

"I know we won't find them here," Dawn muttered, the disgust at her naiveté causing Eden's smile to deepen. "I just thought my dad might like one of those mugs."

Yes, she mused, turning on her side and pulling the covers closer around her shoulders. Dawn's thoughtful desire to provide her father with a present had shown a burgeoning need for closeness in their steadily growing relationship, and she had been filled with satisfaction. Dawn was going to be all right! On this thought Eden sighed. Her lips curved tenderly as she drifted into sleep, unaware that the image of Steven's pleasure when he received his child's gift superseded Dawn's face in her dreams.

CHAPTER SIX

Slowly Eden wandered around the building site, excitement running through her as she observed the extent of the week's work. Steven had every available carpenter and electrician in the area working nearly around the clock, but even so, she was still surprised by the amount accomplished each day.

Today was Saturday, and although technically she shouldn't be working, she couldn't resist the opportunity to check things over without disrupting the workers. Frankly, her presence today was more in the nature of a chance to gloat unobserved, she realized. Throwing her head back, she sniffed the smell of freshly cut wood, which blended with the scent of pine and the more pungent odor of resin.

Her rubber-soled feet strode eagerly through the building debris, her eyes seeing not the bare, skeletal construction, but the finished resort. To Eden, the project as it would be in the future was more of a reality than the incomplete chaos around her. Her own artistry had stipulated the placement of every board, and she felt a sense of awe at the knowledge that this project would prove to be a reflection of her talent.

Since coming to Lake Shasta, she had modified her

original design to a very large degree. The resort was to be spread over several acres, with outlying cabins surrounding a central complex, which consisted of a main lodge for those who preferred a room-service atmosphere. Eden had utilized every tree and shrub possible to hide the cabins within natural greenery, giving complete privacy to those who wished it.

She felt that the unvarying grayness of concrete, the everyday clatter of urban noises, the smog and fume-filled air, soon had those who lived in cities screaming with the need to escape. She herself had often felt that way, trapped within the exacting demands of efficiency, unable to escape the unceasing use of the higher nerve centers. Here, though, would be a paradise for those seeking a respite, and she felt as if she would be in direct contact with all the people to come after her. They would never guess, as they slept in the rustic warmth of the cabins she had designed, or enjoyed fishing or boating on the lake, that a part of Eden resided with them. When she left for home, a large slice of her heart would remain behind, and no matter what she did in the future, she was afraid her mind would always wander back to the silent woods, and the brilliant blue clarity of the lake they embraced.

Eden lifted her head, Dawn's voice breaking through her absorption.

"Over here, honey!"

"Eden, oh, Eden!"

Dawn hurled herself in Eden's direction, her small body shaking with sobs. While her arms automatically moved to embrace the child, Eden was shaking her head in bewilderment.

"What is it?" she asked, tilting Dawn's face upward. "What's happened?"

"I—I did what you said," Dawn hiccupped. "I took my pretty card and Daddy's present downstairs, and just to be sure he knew it was for him, I wrote *Daddy* all over the envelope, and . . . and he didn't even bother to open them."

"You left them on the breakfast table?"

"Y-yes, and they were still there when I got up this morning."

"Maybe Daddy wasn't hungry," she soothed. "He probably hasn't even been in the breakfast room. I bet when you go back, he'll be there, and then you can watch while he opens it."

"I'm never going back," Dawn screamed, her eyes filled with the dreaded pain that Eden had hoped never to see again. "I hate him! I wish I'd never gotten him that old mug!"

"Darling, you don't mean that!"

"I do. I do mean it," Dawn whimpered, tightening her grip around Eden's waist. "He . . . he told me that everyone just *thought* you were going to marry him, so they wouldn't say bad things about you, but you can still be my mommy, can't you, Eden?"

"No, honey," she sighed, brushing a light kiss across the child's forehead. So Steven had attempted to explain things to Dawn, she thought, a frown creasing her brow. She had worried about nothing, and at this particular moment she felt she could wring his neck for not telling her. Still, mingling with her anger was relief. At least she could stop dreading the moment when Dawn would question her about her relationship to Steven.

"But you're going to stay here, aren't you? You'll never go away?"

Eden closed her eyes, pain coursing through her. There

had been too many lies in Dawn's young life, she realized, and she couldn't add to the seriousness of this situation by evading the truth.

"Dawn, I'll have to go home someday, even though I don't want to leave you."

"B-but why can't you stay if you want to?"

"Because I have a job to do here," she explained, motioning toward the bare framework rising up out of the chaos around them. "As soon as it's finished, I'll have to go on to the next project. That's how I make my living, honey."

"Then I'm coming with you," Dawn cried, a mutinous slant to her trembling mouth. "I won't stay here with him. I won't!"

Eden had reached the end of her patience. Grasping Dawn's thin, young shoulders within her firm clasp, she looked down at her. "Now, listen here, young lady," she ordered, accompanying her words with a slight shake. "You haven't even given your father a chance to love you, and I'm not standing for any more of it. The only reason he let me stay here and work was because he knew you liked me."

"I love you," she sobbed, her eyes deep pools of misery in her little white face. She was shocked out of her own self-absorption by Eden's sternness, just as Eden had hoped, but the knowledge didn't ease the pain she felt at inflicting further hurt on the child.

"I love you too," she whispered, framing Dawn's wet cheeks in her palms. "Oh, God," she gasped, her own eyes widening in anguish as she jerked Dawn once again into the circle of her longing arms. "Don't cry, please don't. I promise I'll write to you, and I'll come and visit every

92

chance I get. Maybe Daddy will even let you come and visit me, once he doesn't have to be afraid of losing you."

Eden waited in silence for Dawn's reaction to her words, hoping against hope that the subtle message she was trying to convey would get through to her. Eventually her patience was rewarded as Dawn pulled her head back, her face a mixture of shock and disbelief.

"What do you mean, Eden? Daddy's not afraid of anything."

"He is, you know," she insisted. "Oh, I don't mean he's not brave, just that he sometimes feels afraid inside. You can understand that, can't you?"

Dawn shook her head, and Eden tenderly brushed back her disordered hair with a shaking hand.

"He's afraid of losing the only person in the world he cares about. I think you know who that is, don't you?"

A flush darkened Dawn's cheeks, and she evaded Eden's searching glance. This time her head bobbed up and down, and Eden smiled. She felt a giant abyss had just been crossed in Dawn's life, and was at once more optimistic for the future. She prayed she could talk Steven into letting Dawn spend some time with her. Although she often thought him cold and insensitive, she sensed this was his way of hiding emotions long ago distorted by pain. It was much easier to pretend not to feel at all than to let yourself feel too much. That was the pathway to more hurt, and eventually a person felt he or she just couldn't stand anymore. Wasn't she a good example of that? Only Steven had forced her to open up, to once again allow love to color her life. And he would just have to share the responsibility by sharing his child, she vowed.

Shaking herself out of her reveries, she smiled. "Why don't we walk back to the house and find that father of

93

yours?" she suggested. "Maybe Mrs. Adams will know where he is."

"All right," Dawn agreed, wiping the back of her hands across her eyes before returning Eden's smile. "You . . . you'll stay with me, won't you?"

"While Daddy opens his present?"

Dawn nodded, clutching Eden's hand nervously as they started walking.

"If you want me to. But wouldn't you rather be alone with Daddy?"

"It's not that," Dawn muttered, lowering her head while she kicked at a clump of dirt in the path. "Only I want you too!"

With sadness Eden wondered how many children uttered a plea like Dawn's. She remembered her own childhood, disturbed by fighting parents, but how much worse it had been when they had finally divorced. Then she had become their means of scoring off one another until eventually she had closed off her inner self to both of them. They were each remarried now, her mother living with her lawyer husband in Chicago, her father retired to a villa in Acapulco, and about the only contact she had with either of them was an occasional card.

Possibly that was one of the reasons she had been so careful in the choosing of a husband. She had looked for someone with similar interests, passable looks, but mainly with a strong sense of family obligation. She distrusted her friends' rapturous accounts of their relationships with their boyfriends, determined not to make the mistake her parents had, of thinking a sexual attraction necessarily meant love.

With a sigh Eden's mind wandered back through the years of her marriage. In a way they'd been happy, but she wasn't fooling herself as to the reasons for her contentment. Her main happiness had been centered around Shelley, and John had, over the years, become a necessary appendage. That he, too, loved their child had probably been the only thing holding them together toward the end—that and Eden's self-effacement. John had always known best, his ego demanding constant adulation, and at the time of his death, she remembered, she had begun to feel a great deal was lacking in her life. Poor John! She couldn't help wondering if he had been as happy with their relationship as he had seemed. In the last year of their marriage he had been working later and later hours, spending less time at home than ever before. Could the trap she had begun to feel around her have extended to encompass him too?

Depending solely upon herself for her happiness might not give her all the satisfaction she craved, but it was better than trusting her life to another person. If she was unhappy at times, she had only herself to blame, and she preferred it that way, didn't she?

"Eden, do you think Daddy will read my card?"

They had just reached the front of the house when Dawn spoke, her footsteps faltering uncertainly upon the porch steps.

"I'm sure he will," she smiled, squeezing Dawn's hand reassuringly. "It was a very lovely card. Why do you ask?"

"Oh, no reason," she mumbled, refusing to meet Eden's eyes when they reached the shelter of the porch overhang.

"Honey, is something bothering you?"

"No, of course not," Dawn laughed, reaching out to open the door. "It's only that I—I put *Love* on the card, and I wanted him to read it."

As it turned out, they didn't have to go looking for

Steven. As they entered the breakfast room to make sure the package still lay unopened, he entered from the kitchen. From the look of his dirt-encased boots, their normally shiny patina dulled by a film of reddish dust, he had been working. If the exhaustion Eden saw clouding his features was anything to go by, he hadn't had very much sleep the night before. Maybe he hadn't even been home when she and Dawn had returned. He might have spent all or most of the night with one of those women he had admitted to seeing occasionally, and she felt a tiny flicker of pain at the thought. But it wasn't any business of hers how he spent his nights, or days either, for that matter.

"Hello, you two," he smiled, raking the burnished thickness of his hair back self-consciously. "As you can see, I'm not fit company for the luncheon table. Give me ten minutes to shower and shave, and I'll look a little more presentable."

By now Dawn was bouncing around on the balls of her feet, her face vivid with excitement. Unable to contain herself, she blurted out, "Daddy, there's something for you on your plate."

Steven turned toward Dawn's pointing finger, and as his gaze took in the gaily wrapped parcel, he turned puzzled eyes in Eden's direction.

"It was all Dawn's idea," she smiled softly. "We both bought new clothes yesterday, and she didn't want to leave you out."

"Dawn didn't want . . ." he whispered, his eyes going quickly over his daughter's features. "You bought me a present, honey?"

Dawn nodded, her excitement dulled by shyness. "Are you going to open it, Daddy?"

"You bet I am, sweetheart," he rasped, the muscle pulsing in his jaw telling Eden better than words just how moved he was. Averting her eyes, a lump forming in her throat, she began to leave the room, until a pleading look from Dawn stopped her. Remembering her promise, she held herself immobile with effort, feeling distinctly *de trop* during this first tentative reaching-out between father and daughter.

Tension tightened Eden's neck muscles as Steven's large, work-worn hands tenderly unwrapped the package, and she wasn't a bit surprised to notice the trembling in his fingers as he worked to release the tape without tearing the paper. Eventually he succeeded, lifting the lid of the box and carefully removing the tissue paper around the mug. For long moments he stared at it, turning it over and over in his hands.

Steven turned away abruptly. Moving with a swift stride, he passed through the swinging doors and into the kitchen. Just before the doors swung together, Eden caught a brief glimpse of his strong back, his shoulders hunched as he leaned against the sink.

"Daddy doesn't like my present," Dawn gulped, her voice quivering with anguish.

Placing her hand on the child's head, Eden absently ruffled her hair. "Why don't you wait and see," she urged with a smile. "I think you might be surprised, honey."

At that moment Steven's voice attracted their attention, and both she and Dawn turned startled eyes in his direction. His words were for his daughter, the aroma of coffee emanating from Dawn's gift, which he held carefully between his palms, as if it were made of the finest gold.

"Really, Daddy? You really love my present?"

"More than I've ever loved anything, Punkin, except

97

maybe you. I'll think of you every morning when I have my coffee."

Doubt still shadowed Dawn's eyes as she looked up at her father. "Why didn't you tell me you liked it then?" she questioned, tiny frown lines creasing her brow. "You . . . you just walked away."

Placing the coffee beside him while he perched on the edge of the table, Steven drew Dawn forward. His eyes studied her piquant face, his own expression serious as he cradled her cheeks in his hands.

"Honey, sometimes when someone you love very much gives you a present, it's hard to find the right way to say thank you," he explained, his thumbs caressing the child's cheeks. "I'm sorry if you thought I wasn't happy with your gift. It's just that I—I needed to be by myself for a while."

A radiant smile lighted Dawn's eyes, and she nodded her head in eager understanding. "I know what you mean," she cried, her mouth quirking in a dimpled smile. "That's the way I felt about Pooh Bear, Daddy!"

Eden was amazed by the look of anguish that appeared momentarily in Steven's eyes. She couldn't stand looking at him any longer, and abruptly turned.

What in the world had the child said to cause such a reaction? she wondered. Her curiosity was satisfied when Steven spoke again, and she had to fight to keep her own tears from spilling over.

"You remember Pooh Bear?"

The grating harshness in his voice sent vibrations rippling over Eden's skin as she realized the significance behind the question. From what she'd pieced together, Dawn had been very attached to her father during those early years, before his wife had removed the child from his influence. Because of the trauma she had later suffered, she apparently wiped those early memories from her mind. Instead, her father had become a vaguely sinister figure, a monster created from the sick mind of the mother. Now, though, Dawn's mind was finally unlocking the secrets of the past, and Eden felt like crying from sheer joy. She was sure that one happy memory would lead to another, and soon the shadows obscuring Dawn's image of her father would be dispelled forever.

"I have a surprise for you and Eden too." As Steven's voice penetrated her concentration, Eden looked upward, her face questioning. A ruddy tide of color darkened Steven's cheekbones. With his arm around Dawn, he approached, and one finger rose to flick the underside of her chin.

"Trying to catch flies?" Steven asked Eden.

The sound of Dawn's giggle was drowned out by Steven's low, masculine laughter, and Eden's lips snapped indignantly together at once.

"I just can't imagine why you'd want to get me a present," she muttered, trying to control her own intensifying color.

"I didn't *get* you a present, I *made* one," he teased, his mouth quirking as he suppressed a smile. "Come on!"

Eden followed him from the kitchen without uttering another word, her own curiosity almost as great as that of the child skipping excitedly at her side. Glancing up at Steven's face as they negotiated the uneven terrain, her breath caught in her throat. *He looks like a little boy,* she thought, shocked by a sudden wave of tenderness. His eyes were alight with inner excitement, his mouth losing all the repressed harshness she had always associated with him.

"There!" He turned to them with tender triumph written clearly in his expression as they halted at the base of the small clearing she and Dawn loved so much. "Now the two of you can watch your doe and her fawn from a perfect vantage point. From inside this hide, you'll be close enough to reach out and touch them."

With a squeal Dawn raced toward the wooden foliage-covered structure, quickly disappearing inside. For long moments Eden remained speechless, a growing ache building in her throat.

"Tears?" he murmured, his hands framing her face with exquisite tenderness.

"Why?" she choked, suddenly seeing him with new eyes. "You . . . I thought you disapproved of us coming here to care for the doe."

His expression sobered. "I don't know," he whispered, a bemused frown creasing his brow as he stared down at her. Slowly his thumbs brushed her cheeks, wiping away her tears with as much gentleness as he would use to a child. "Ever since the first day you came here, I haven't recognized myself. You've slowly but surely undermined the man I thought myself to be, until now I find myself wondering how you'll react to everything I do. I think that demands a forfeit, don't you?"

Slowly his head lowered, his mouth brushing against hers with heart-wrenching sensitivity. His kiss was brief, demanding no response, and as their lips clung and then parted, she was left staring at his mouth with enthralled concentration. She felt something flaring to life inside of her, an exquisite warmth radiating from the deepest part of her being.

"Steven . . ."

The realization that she had misjudged him made her utterance of his name more of a cry for forgiveness. With self-denigration she faced the truth about herself, and it wasn't something she was proud of admitting. From the beginning she had been using Steven's bitterness and disillusion with women to guard herself against him. No, she admitted wryly. The only one she was guarding against was herself. She was afraid of becoming immersed within his strength of character, afraid of opening up and flowering in the warmth of a sexual attraction that left her vulnerable.

Yesterday, when Steven had accused her of seducing James, her anger had been submerged by pain. Strangely enough, she hadn't known until this moment why his censure had hurt her so badly, and the knowledge appalled her. With Steven, she couldn't seem to control her responses—or even her will. She had never allowed her life to be governed by emotions; she was afraid of something as ephemeral as passion. She had always been in control, planning her life with sensible precision. With Steven it was different—a difference she was scared to even attempt to grasp.

"Eden?"

"W-what?"

"Nothing, just Eden," he murmured, a slow smile curving his lips.

Closing her eyes didn't succeed in preventing the slumbrous flicker of his to pierce her soul. The warmth of his glance was still there, dancing behind her fluttering lids. She stiffened as his mouth brushed across each closed lid, her whole body aching with the suppressed need to hold him closer.

"Gentle little doe eyes," he murmured, his voice sounding as shaken as she felt.

At Dawn's return Eden was grateful for the opportunity

101

to break the spell surrounding them. Returning to the house, only Dawn's chatter did anything to alleviate the tense silence between herself and Steven. She entered the kitchen and poured herself a cup of fresh coffee with shaking hands. She could hear Dawn's piping voice in the background, successfully creating a diversion from her introspection. As Steven's deep tones mingled with Dawn's, she heard her name mentioned and turned toward them, at last feeling some of her normal control returning.

"I was just asking Dawn if she'd like to go out in the boat for the rest of the day, and she wants you to go with us, Eden."

"Please, Eden," Dawn squealed, running over and throwing her arms around Eden's waist. "Daddy said we can take a picnic, and maybe there'll be enough left over to feed the deer."

Opening her mouth to refuse, she was interrupted by Steven.

"Dawn won't enjoy herself nearly as much if she's worried about leaving you at home," he said, getting slowly to his feet. "Go and pack your bathing suits and all the other junk you women find indispensable on an outing of this kind, and I'll scrounge around here for something to eat."

She knew by his autocratic tone that it wouldn't do her much good to argue, and, besides, she found the prospect of a day on the lake too tempting to refuse. Leading a giggling Dawn by the hand, she contented herself with sending Steven a speaking glance from under lowered brows, scowling even more fiercely when he laughed.

A shimmering heat haze distorted Eden's vision as she

lay sunbathing in the back of Steven's mini day cruiser. When she had first caught sight of the boat, she remembered how difficult it had been to suppress her gasp of admiration. Gleaming white trimmed in burgundy, the luxurious craft seemed her idea of heaven as it rocked gently at its moorings. Steven's smile had been teasing as he helped her aboard, her eagerness apparently amusing him. She had been determined to hold herself aloof in an attempt to show her displeasure at being ordered around, but found it virtually impossible. It was difficult maintaining a grudge on such a perfect day, especially since she possessed an irritatingly forgiving nature.

Dawn's squeals added a background for Steven's heartier laugh, and Eden smiled sleepily. From the sound of all the splashing activity beside the boat, she surmised that Dawn was having the time of her life. She really should go back in herself, she thought, squirming uncomfortably from the force of the sun's rays burning into her back. Just a few moments longer . . .

With a gasp Eden jumped, rolling over onto her back and sitting upright in one fluid movement.

"You brute, I was almost asleep," she muttered, shivering as the cold water Steven had poured over her dripped down her back.

"There was no almost about it," he grinned, lowering his dripping form beside her. "You were snoring like mad when I climbed over the side."

"I never snore," she retorted, failing to disguise the telltale quirk tilting the corner of her mouth. Steven laughed, stretching his legs indolently until a muscular brown thigh was almost touching Eden's slender equivalent. His closeness made her nervous, and she tried to think of a way to put a little more distance between them in such a confined area.

As if able to read her mind, his eyes narrowed devilishly, and to her consternation he supported himself on one arm while reaching across her to open the locker at her side.

"Do you want something?" His breath wafted warmly across her face as he spoke, and although the words sounded innocent enough, she couldn't mistake the sensual inflection in his voice. Startled, her eyes locked with his, and she moistened her suddenly dry lips with the tip of her tongue.

"No, thank you," she whispered, her eyes widening nervously.

All teasing left his face, which had stilled alarmingly. For long moments his gaze raked her features consideringly, until she lowered her eyes in confusion. As he uttered a muffled imprecation and threw himself on his back beside her, she didn't know whether to be relieved or not. She could feel a palpable tension emanating from his recumbent form, and the knowledge made her more uncomfortable in his presence than usual.

"W-would you like me to get you a beer?" she offered, attempting to once more restore their earlier harmony.

"What if I told you there was something else I wanted?"

Concentrating solely on trying to control her suddenly erratic heartbeat, she completely missed the strained inflection in his words and turned toward him with a puzzled frown.

"Are you still hungry? I could get you something . . ."

"I'm hungry," he smiled, his eyes glinting wickedly up at her, "but not for food."

Too late, Eden realized the direction of his thoughts. Before she could move, his hand cupped the back of her neck. She was thrown off-balance when he exerted pressure, her arms flailing in a futile effort to save herself. All too soon she was sprawled across the hairy expanse of sun-kissed chest, the breath knocked out of her from the force of her descent.

Opening her mouth to protest was a mistake. His mouth covered hers with sensual force, his hands moving to shield her head from the wooden deck as he rolled her over onto her back. Pushing at his waist did no good. Her hands slid maddeningly over his dampened flesh as she struggled to free herself from his crushing weight.

Twisting her body to gain better leverage, she managed to release her leg from the entwining length of his. Praying her aim was accurate, she swung her foot, feeling a momentary sense of satisfaction when his pained grunt was lost inside her throbbing mouth.

Steven's head lifted, and she felt remorseful when she noticed the lurking pain in his eyes. Surely she hadn't hurt him that much?

"Oh, Eden," he whispered, his mouth twisting convulsively while a muscle pulsed in his jaw. "Will you ever stop fighting me long enough to accept that it could be good between us? We've both been hurt by life, but does that mean we must exist without really allowing ourselves to feel again? Please, honey! Knock down that wall you've built between us and let yourself see me, really see the man and not the image you've created as a defense. I have strengths and weaknesses like everyone else, and right now, God help me, you're my downfall. If you can't believe my words, then let my body show you what I feel!"

His whole frame trembled against the warm length of

hers. She could summon no resistance against him, the vibrant need in his whispered words meeting and merging with an urge inside herself that demanded compliance. The firm, sensuous lines of a mouth softened miraculously by desire hovered tantalizingly close and, with a muffled sob, her own mouth rose to meet it.

His lips twisted and moved across hungrily throbbing flesh, teasing and tormenting her until she responded to its movements with a mindless pleasure she had never before in her life felt. With a boldness that shocked her, she lifted her hands, running the palms over the crisp hairs of his chest, loving the feel of his skin against her sensitive fingertips. Up and down she stroked in growing frenzy, from the base of his heavily throbbing throat to below his navel. With teasing insistence she probed the tiny orifice, her fingers alive with the desire to explore every inch of available skin.

With a shuddering groan Steven tensed, his hand covering hers even as his mouth trailed moistly over her chin to nestle against the wildly beating pulse in her throat. Exerting pressure, he slipped her hand beneath the dampened waistband of his swimming trunks, gasping as her touch grazed the throbbing core of his manhood.

"Oh, God!" he choked, instinctively arching his body in unmistakable rhythm. "Touch me . . . hold me!"

At the first touch of her fingers against his aroused need, Eden froze, becoming suddenly aware of the danger she was inviting. Her fingers no longer teased and probed, their movements stilled as shock rippled through her. She opened her eyes as Steven tugged unsuccessfully at the knot holding her bikini top together over her breasts and almost cried out at the savage concentration on his face.

How in the world had they gone so far so quickly? Had

it been his tenderness, his sensitivity, that had dulled her usual common sense, or the burning ache for completion she felt flowering hotly through her bloodstream? At the moment she neither knew nor cared who, of the two of them, had done the seducing. All she knew was that she had to stop the progress of their lovemaking, for both their sakes. After having gone this far, her resistance would make him furious, but she couldn't subdue the principles of a lifetime by giving in to a purely physical need.

Taking him by surprise, she pushed violently against his chest, at the same moment rolling from beneath him until she sat, her head resting on her drawn-up knees.

"Was this a calculated punishment, or did you just want to enjoy the sight of me in agony?"

As she heard the bitterness in his voice, her wildly fluctuating emotions settled with aching pain somewhere in the region of her chest. She shook her head in a violent motion, unable to raise her eyes and see the condemnation she knew lurked in his face.

"Why, Eden?" he groaned. "For God's sake, what are you trying to do to me . . . to us?"

Lifting her head, she cringed at the derision in his eyes. She felt naked under the merciless inspection, stripped even of the minute blue-flowered bikini covering her shaking form.

"You don't understand," she whispered, her eyes pleading for understanding. "I can't . . . can't . . ."

"You can't or won't?"

She didn't hear his approach until he was crouched beside her, startled from her intense inspection of the deck by the touch of his hand running tenderly across her arm. She couldn't suppress an aroused gasp from escaping her trembling lips any more than she could hide from the knowledge that her whole body cried out to her to return to his arms.

"Don't hide from the truth, Eden," he murmured, sliding his hand across her collarbone until his fingertips teased the softly curling hairs at the nape of her neck. "You know as well as I do that a moment ago you wanted it as badly as I did!"

Oh, God. She had to think! There had to be some way to end this torment. Her mind refused to function with the temptation of his body so near, remembering only the feel of his warm flesh beneath her sensitive fingers, the silken body hair against her.

"I—I don't like post mortems," she stammered, flinching away from his touch. "What just happened is over and done with, and I for one have no intention of repeating the experience."

"I want you, Eden," he said, his mouth curving in a wry, yet strangely appealing smile. "And you want me!"

"That's not true," she lied, realizing that only by angering him could she hope for a reprieve from a situation nearly out of control. Taking a deep breath, she forced herself to meet his eyes, trying to summon a coldness in her voice she was far from feeling. "I know this will be hard for your masculine ego to accept, but I have no thoughts about you at all. What happened was instinctive. I'm only human, after all. But I draw the line at grasping at pleasure solely for pleasure's sake. Now, let me up before I scream," she demanded. "You wouldn't want to have to explain this situation to Dawn, would you?"

Calling on whatever reserves of courage left to her, she got to her feet, clenching her fists at her sides as his hands shot out to capture her shoulders in a bruising grip.

"What are you threatening, Eden?"

Ashamed at using an innocent child as a means to an end, she slowly withdrew from his clasp. Slumping onto the padded bench that lined the sides of the cruiser, she winced from the heat.

It was a good thing Steven had moored the craft in the small, rock-encrusted cove, she thought. She couldn't have stood very much movement right now. Her stomach was turning somersaults as it was. Depression settled over her as she gazed into the distance.

Dawn was playing on the cove's shore, one of many which dotted the miles of lakefront with welcome seclusion. Eden's eyes were burning with the attempt at suppressing her tears as she watched the child scramble over rocky earth toward the stand of trees girding the top of the outcrop.

An inner voice taunted her, encouraging her to take whatever Steven chose to offer her. For the first time, she admitted to herself that he was right. She was running from him, hiding an inner response to him so strong that she despaired of ever being free again. Yet, without love on his part, or even affection, what he was asking her to give was wrong. He wouldn't be content with simply possessing her body. She knew, with a shuddering certainty, that he would demand more from her than it was possible to tolerate.

With a sigh she turned her face in the direction of the now stern-faced man standing by the low railing of the boat. He again looked as he had the first time she saw him, she realized—cold and unapproachable. Only now, God help her, she knew his sternness hid a man almost too sensitive to the vagaries of human nature, a man easily hurt, who had built a defensive shield around his emotions to hide his longing for warmth and tenderness. Slowly that shield was cracking, but her own growing weakness toward him frightened her, increasing her certainty that she wasn't strong enough to give him what he needed and yet still manage to retain her own identity. Glancing at him now, in low-slung black bathing trunks which did nothing to hide the magnificent angles of his body, she had to steel herself from showing any reaction to his sheer animal magnetism.

"I'm not threatening you," she explained quietly. "But I think it will be better between you and your daughter without me around to complicate things. I know I planned on staying until the project was further along, but that's no longer important to me."

"And Dawn, isn't she important to you any longer?"

"You're not being fair," she protested. "You know how much I love her, but don't you see? She's becoming too attached to me as it is. If I don't leave soon, she might not be able to accept it when I do eventually return home."

"What makes you think she'll accept it now?"

"I've promised her I'll write to her, and she seemed fairly receptive to the idea," she explained, lowering her head to stare at the clenched hands resting in her lap. Clearing her throat, she once again raised shadowed eyes to his. "I—I told her I hoped you might let her visit me."

"You did what?"

In two swift strides he was beside her, his large hands clasping her shoulders and hauling her to her feet.

"I—I know it was wrong of me to mention it to Dawn without discussing it with you first, but she was upset, and I wanted to comfort her."

"You've made damn sure that no matter what happens, you won't lose Dawn, haven't you?"

"It's t-true that I don't want to go out of her life forever, but I didn't do it intentionally. You've got to believe me," she cried, appalled by his suspicion of her motives. "Please, I—I know what it is to lose a child, and no matter what you think, I wouldn't have deliberately tried to separate you from Dawn."

Eden thought she saw a brief flare of pity darken his eyes, but the expression was so fleeting, she might have imagined it. Instead, she felt herself being pulled inexorably forward until only inches separated his body from hers.

"There is a solution, you know," he murmured, his breath fanning the top of her hair.

"If there is," she gasped, the warmth emanating from his body causing prickles of awareness to ripple over her chilled flesh. "If there is, then I certainly haven't discovered it!"

"Haven't you?" Their glances locked, and a feeling of dread shivered through her.

"I don't understand," she whispered.

"You can stay with Dawn. All you have to do is be willing to carry our farcical engagement toward a logical conclusion."

"If you mean what I think, then you're crazy," she protested, shaking her head violently. "I have a career I've worked hard for, one I have no intention of giving up."

"I'll set you up in an office in Redding," he said, his voice coolly matter-of-fact. "You could build a bigger name for yourself here than buried in your present firm."

Eden could feel the blood pounding in her head, and what was worse, she could feel herself weakening. He was seducing her with words calculated to appeal to every clamoring instinct within her, and he knew it—the devil! The trap was closing around her, a loveless cage that would enable her to stay close to the child as long as she was willing to barter herself.

"If you're trying to impress me with all this maidenly hesitation, don't bother," he said, his head lowering until his mouth made contact with the tender flesh just beneath her ear. "Using James to make me jealous was a stroke of genius. It made me realize that even without love, I'm primitive enough to want to tie you to me in any way possible—including bribery. But you've known how to get to me every step of the way, haven't you?" he groaned, his tongue licking against the inside of her ear. "Oh, God," he muttered. "Marry me, sweetheart, and you'll have it all, the money to establish yourself at the top of your profession, and Dawn."

CHAPTER SEVEN

Eden jerked away from the provoking warmth of Steven's mouth. She was reeling with outrage, conflicting emotions giving her wide eyes a luminous quality as she stared into his face. Twin flags colored her cheeks a bright red as their glances locked in silent battle, and the leaping of her pulses aroused by his nearness left her shaking.

A vision of herself and Steven rose in her mind, triggered by his suggestion that she become his wife. Remembering the insolent insinuation of his last words, she silently castigated herself for even briefly allowing her imagination to cloud her common sense. There could be no future in an arrangement such as the one he was advocating, and she lost no time in telling him how she felt.

"What the hell do you mean, no future?" he rasped, his hands tightening on her arms in frustration. "The way I see it, you've manipulated both my daughter and me in this direction, and now you want to back out. Why? Because I might convince you to act like a woman?"

"That's not true," she stormed, sickened by the image he held of her. "If there's anyone to be blamed, it certainly isn't me."

"Don't be childish," he snapped. "No matter who's at fault, it doesn't change the circumstances. The fact remains that against my better judgment you've become a part of our lives, and I see no reason for either Dawn or myself to be denied."

"In other words, you're prepared to sacrifice your comfortable existence for the sake of your little girl? That's very big of you, but no thanks. There's one person you haven't considered in all your fine plans—me! Contrary to your beliefs, I have no intention of tying myself to a man who would make me feel good for only one thing . . . two, if you count looking after Dawn. No! I'll begin packing tonight, and be out of here by tomorrow afternoon."

"You're telling me you'd take the child but not the father. Strange," he murmured, his eyes holding hers. "I somehow got the impression that you wouldn't find sharing my bed much of a hardship."

"I—I have no plans for sharing your bed," she gasped, the ready color flushing her cheeks. "That's all you want anyway," she said, her eyes filled with scorn. "What's the matter, are you tired of finding your pleasure in town? Does the idea of having a woman readily on hand appeal to you?"

"I get your drift," he muttered, flinging her from him in disgust. "Don't worry, Eden. If the idea of my lovemaking is so repulsive, we'll alter the arrangement."

Before she could utter the scathing denunciation aching for release, Steven had jumped over the side of the cruiser, his body hitting the water in a graceful arc.

The powerful cleaving strokes of his arms barely disturbed the mirrored surface of the lake as he went over to where Dawn was playing. While Eden watched, he walked onto the shore, the sunlight revealing the gleaming perfection of his body in explicit detail. *It isn't fair for any one man to possess quite so much physical attraction,* she thought resentfully. At that moment he turned and caught her staring at him, and although the distance was too great to see the expression in his eyes, she suspected they were openly mocking her apparent fascination.

With frustration Eden turned away, busying herself with tidying the cruiser. She felt disoriented, unable to concentrate on even the simplest of tasks, and with a groan headed for the small bathroom below. She splashed cold water over her heated face and studied her reflection in the mirror over the basin, grimacing at the flush still coloring her cheeks.

Although the pounding of her heart had lessened, the throb of pain at her temples that was beginning told her better than words how upset she was. Deciding to stay below, her reluctant footsteps carried her over to the padded benches just outside of the tiny galley. Resting her head against a gaily patterned cushion, she closed her eyes, thoughts of her recent confrontation with Steven causing her to shiver with reaction. The leather of the bench was cool against her back as she lay there, trying to come to terms with Steven's insulting proposal.

In the distance she heard Dawn's laughter floating on the still, clear air, and she flinched at the sound. The violence of her recent emotions had almost clouded the real issue between her and Steven—the child! If she stayed and married Steven, she would never have to leave Dawn, a nagging little voice taunted from the back of her mind. The sudden hope spiraling within her breast died shamefully as an image of herself locked within Steven's careless embrace rose from the depths of her subconscious.

Wincing at the memory, she shook her head, drawing in her breath in a sobbing gasp. She couldn't sell herself,

115

her whole future, for Dawn—no matter how much she loved her. To Steven she would become little better than a glorified nanny during the day, and a convenient body to enjoy when darkness fell. His attitude today showed her clearly how much he despised her as a person, and she couldn't live with the indignity of losing her independence, not to mention her self-respect.

God! What a mess she had gotten herself into, she mourned. She would die inside if she had to leave Dawn now. She couldn't bear it. Yet, she couldn't live here always. She had a life apart from Steven and Dawn, a career, and as much of a hollow substitute it now seemed to her, it was all she did have. She didn't belong here, would never belong. Like Dawn with her crippled deer, Eden knew she would now have to pay for the loving by once again suffering the loss of separation.

The laughter was coming closer. With an inarticulate cry, Eden jumped to her feet, reaching beneath the bench to the hollow compartment that held her jeans and shirt. With shaking fingers, she pulled on her clothes, the slight rocking motion the boat made when Steven and Dawn boarded letting her know she was just in time. Biting down hard on the fullness of her lower lip as she contemplated having to face Steven again, she tucked the trailing ends of her multihued madras shirt into the band at her waist. Taking a deep breath in an attempt to steady her rioting emotions, she walked up on shaky legs.

When Dawn turned from talking to her father and spotted Eden, she ended the conversation abruptly. Running forward with damp pigtails flying, she catapulted herself into Eden's arms.

"Guess what?" she cried, her face alight with eagerness as she pulled back from Eden's encircling arms. Not wait-

116

ing for Eden's answer, she began telling her of the three does that had come almost within touching distance to eat the bread she had provided.

Although uncomfortably aware of Steven's watching eyes, Eden must have made all the appropriate responses, because it was obvious Dawn didn't suspect Eden's inner turmoil. Unable to resist the temptation, she raised her eyes to where he was leaning negligently against the rail and immediately wished she hadn't. Droplets of moisture gleamed on his sun-browned body, and unwillingly she remembered the touch of his dampened flesh against her palms. Raising her eyes from the diamond speckles dotting the darkened hair on his chest, she met his narrow-eyed glance with a sense of shock. A ripple of blatant desire coursed through her veins as Steven raised a can of beer to his lips. His eyes never left hers as his throat moved convulsively. Lowering the can, a slow smile curved his mouth, the message in his eyes making a mockery of the pure and uncomplicated recital by Dawn.

Clinging to that young voice as to a lifeline, Eden withdrew her attention from Steven, framing the child's face within shaking fingers.

"You didn't get too close to the deer, did you, sweetheart?"

"No, I remembered what you told me, Eden."

"And just what was it Eden told you this time?" Steven drawled. Dawn missed the mocking insinuation in his voice, and turned to answer him with youthful enthusiasm.

"She told me never to get too close to a mother deer or her baby, because she could think I'm going to hurt the baby, and might kick me," she explained, her words tripping over themselves until she was gasping for breath.

"Very wise," he said, his sardonic glance taking in the clothes now covering Eden's bikini. "But then, our Eden's smart about a great many things, especially how a parent might react when backed into a corner."

Eden knew what he was referring to, and hated him for continuing his campaign in Dawn's presence. Although to be honest, the meaning behind his words went right over the child's head. She only heard him refer to "our Eden," and that was enough to send her flying in his direction.

Hugging his waist, Dawn laughed in joyous abandon, and Steven's face wore a slightly startled expression.

"Hey, what's the hug for?" he asked, running his hand caressingly over Dawn's head and tugging playfully at a sopping pigtail.

"I'm just glad you love Eden too," she giggled, giving his waist another squeeze. "Now she can stay with us and never go away!"

Eden stifled a choked exclamation, raising tortured eyes in his direction. With dismay she noticed the harshly forbidding cast to his chiseled features, realizing he blamed her for the innocent conclusion Dawn had reached from *his* words! A sense of defeat assailed her as she saw the warning gleam in his eyes. She felt helpless against the implacable force of his will, unable to escape the trap she felt closing around her.

"I—I think we'd better start back," she stammered, motioning to a yawning Dawn with a trembling hand. "It's been rather a long day in more ways than one," she concluded, tilting her chin in a defiant attempt to beat him at his own game.

Seating Dawn where she could watch him, Steven began coiling the rope hanging over the end rail, using an economy of movement to reel in the leaded anchor that kept the craft from drifting onto the rocks dotting the shore.

"A very long day," he agreed, finishing his task and walking toward Eden with a self-possession she wished she could emulate. "But an enlightening one!"

She couldn't help wondering just what he meant by his remark. Was he conjecturing about his mistaken character analysis, or had he sensed the tremendous physical response she hadn't been able to hide? As if her thoughts weren't disconcerting enough, she found herself dodging his surefooted approach with something resembling panic. The sardonic twist to his lips as he moved past her only increased her embarrassment, because contrary to her expectations, he made no move to touch her.

Feeling foolish, she sat beside Dawn, who immediately leaned her head tiredly against her breast. As the cruiser picked up speed, Eden watched the curling spume from the propellers as Steven steered the craft across the rippling waves caused by other boats. She noticed there were still a few diehard water-skiers battling the rapidly settling darkness, and she sympathized with their desire to catch every available minute of what had amounted to almost perfect weather.

Staring downward once again at the deep funnel trailing behind the boat, she sighed. She envied those people their uncomplicated enjoyment. She couldn't help wishing that her own day, which had started so pleasantly, hadn't ended in yet another confrontation with Steven. She found it very difficult to contemplate much more of his denigrating suspicions, and almost absentmindedly her arms tightened defensively around the sleeping child in her arms. Staring down at Dawn's face, angelic in repose, she felt the anguish building within her. She wondered if this would be the last time she would be able to hold the little girl close, because she was determined to follow her decision to leave tomorrow. There was so little time left, although Dawn didn't realize it yet, and with slicing pain Eden feathered a light kiss across the soft cheek.

While Steven secured the craft at its mooring, Eden walked up the path slowly, her arm around Dawn. She felt achy, as if her body were suffering from a surfeit of exercise. As they drew within sight of the house she almost groaned with relief, because she didn't think her trembling legs would have carried her much farther.

Her mind was nearly blank with exhaustion as she helped Dawn bathe away the grime from their outing. The child was half-asleep on her feet, and Eden couldn't help but be glad for her silence. Tucking the covers securely around her willingly reclining body, Eden noticed the eyes already closing in sleep with a tender smile.

"G'night, Eden," she mumbled, curling her slight form in a tight ball beneath the covers.

"Good night, sweetheart," she whispered, bending down to kiss her lightly. "Happy dreams."

Moving like a zombie, Eden reached the seclusion of her own room. Automatically switching on the light, she surveyed the familiar surroundings with a sense of dismay. Knowing if she waited until the morning she might very easily change her mind, she began the unenviable task of packing her belongings. At last the dresser was cleared, the closet empty, and with a frozen expression, she firmly closed the clasps on her suitcases. The only things missing were her toilet articles, which she would need in the morning, and the clothes she had chosen to travel in. As for what she was wearing now, she wanted never to see them again. They would hold too many memories of the terrible pain of this moment, and she would discard them without a qualm in the morning, she vowed.

Fighting an ever-increasing depression, Eden stripped the offensive garments from her body, uncharacteristically leaving them in the middle of the floor as she walked into the bathroom. Hoping a hot shower would alleviate her increasing tension, she forced herself not to think of the enormity of the step she had just taken, closing her eyes against the pounding spray in an attempt to isolate herself from thoughts of the future.

After wiping the moisture from her body, she wrapped the bath towel around her and took the blow dryer from its case. *Thank goodness for modern conveniences,* she thought with a wry twist to her lips. She was going to have enough trouble sleeping tonight, without the added discomfort of wet hair.

Endearingly curling locks framed the paleness of her face, the slight sprinkling of freckles across her nose making her grimace at herself in the mirror. She found it hard to understand how Steven could hold the opinion of her that he did, when at the moment she looked little older than Dawn, and as far as she was concerned, a lot less capable of plotting to attract any man, let alone Steven Lassiter.

Dropping her towel in the wicker hamper beside the basin, she grabbed her simple, terry-cloth robe from the hook on the door. Belting it firmly at the waist, she decided to wait until the morning to clean the bathroom, her only thought now one of forgetting her troubles in sleep. She had just turned down the covers on her bed when she jumped nervously, realizing with dread that the sound that had aroused her from her lethargy was a fist hammering forcefully on her sitting-room door.

She walked as far as the archway into the other room and stopped abruptly, her heart pounding as she watched the door open and Steven enter. For what seemed an eternity she stared at him, unable to tear her gaze from the livid fury marring his face. Dear God, what in the world had she done now? she thought, forcing herself to walk farther into the room.

"What d-do you want?

She could have killed herself for ever asking such a leading question as his gaze raked her unmercifully, making her only too conscious of her own nakedness beneath the short robe.

"Can't you guess?"

"Look, I'm tired, and not in the mood to play guessing games," she retorted, her rather shaky courage helped by knowing herself innocent of all of his imaginings. "I know you're my employer, but that doesn't give you the right to make yourself free with my rooms, and they are mine, at least until tomorrow."

She felt relieved when his head turned from his intent appraisal of her defenseless body, but not for long. When his glance encountered her valises tucked away in the corner by the closet, a new nervousness assailed her.

"What are those for—effect?"

The sneer in his voice was unmistakable, and Eden's eyes reflected her confusion. For some reason the sight of her suitcases appeared to be making Steven even angrier than before, and she was at a loss to figure out why. Of all the rude, inconsistent . . . Making mental mincemeat of him wasn't going to help her very much, she thought, but it certainly made her feel better. She couldn't help giving utterance to a low, unamused laugh, but when she heard Steven curse violently, she immediately wished she could take back the sound.

"You find all of this funny?"

"N-no, of course not," she stammered, shivering at the low-voiced threat behind his words. When he uttered the question, he had gestured with his hand, and for the first time she noticed that he held something, something that looked like a letter or a card. Of course! It was the card Dawn had made him to accompany his present. She frowned, wondering why he should bother bringing it to her room. He must have recently opened it, because in the excitement she was sure it had been overlooked. Neither she nor Dawn had thought to tell him it was there, buried beneath the tissue paper which had protected the mug.

Plastering her brightest smile on her face, she gestured toward the slightly crumpled blue envelope.

"What a good thing you found it," she mumbled. "Dawn seemed worried earlier that you wouldn't read it. She told me she put *Love* on the card, and I know she worked quite a long time on it, although that might have just been a ploy to avoid bedtime."

She knew she was babbling; she could hear her voice in her own ears sounding strained, but she couldn't seem to help it. Something in the way he was looking at her in grim-lipped silence was making her incredibly nervous, almost as though she were on the defensive. For heaven's sake, she thought, disgusted with herself. She had nothing to feel guilty about, so why in the world couldn't she seem to stop trembling?

To her dismay Steven began walking toward her with slow, measured footsteps. Determined not to follow her instincts and run, she stood her ground, waiting stiffly until he stood in front of her. To her amazement he hand-ed her the card, and she looked up at him in bewilderment.

"Go on," he ordered, words barely audible through clenched teeth. "Open it. Read what she wrote."

Fingers shaking, Eden took the card from the envelope. Scanning the contents, a shocked exclamation escaped her. All that really registered were the words, "With love and kisses, from Mommy and Dawn." Oh, no! So Dawn hadn't been eager for her father to read the card. Quite the contrary! After talking to Eden this morning, her worry over whether Eden thought her father would read the card had been based on guilt over what she had written. That's why she had appeared so nervous, hanging back when Eden would have entered the house . . . and probably why she had gotten her to promise not to leave. *Oh, darling! You've certainly set the cat among the pigeons this time!* How in the world was she going to convince Steven that she had had nothing to do with Dawn's literary efforts?

Marshalling her thoughts with him towering above her wasn't the easiest thing she'd ever done, but somehow she had to convince him of her innocence. Feeling her neck was already stretched as far as it could go, she saw no reason not to tighten the noose. To her way of thinking, the situation couldn't be worse, and she had nothing left to lose by defending herself.

"Look, I know what you're thinking, but you're wrong," she retorted, tilting her head belligerently. "I provided Dawn with the writing materials, but I swear to you I never saw what she wrote. The card was personal. I know you don't think much of me, but I draw the line at snooping into anyone's letters. And another thing"—she choked, her own anger rising with the sense of injustice assailing her—"y-you should be glad that Dawn is bothering to write to you at all. It's a sweet and loving card, no matter how she chose to sign it!"

"Mmmm," Steven murmured, reaching out with a lazy hand and cupping the back of her neck. "I especially liked the love and kisses part," he taunted, pulling her forward and tilting her head back with his other hand.

"You're mad," she croaked, trying to back away, and gasping audibly when his hand slid down her back to settle firmly within the vulnerable little dimple marking the end of her spine.

"Furious," he admitted, his mouth curving in a sensual smile which nearly stopped her breath.

"I—I didn't mean it that way," she gasped, twisting to evade the mouth below her ear, which was wrecking havoc with her nervous system.

"Why don't you stop fighting me and admit you want this as much as I do, honey?"

If anything was geared to bring her more surely to her senses, it was the deliberate calculation of his words. Pushing against his chest with both hands, she glared up at him, her eyes luminous with the force of her shattered emotions.

"Can't you get it through your thick skull that I don't want you, no matter what Dawn chooses to hope for?"

As soon as she spoke, she realized the enormity of what she had done. Far from making him release her, Steven's hold tightened, and she was forced against his body violently.

"You little witch," he snarled, grabbing her hair in his hand and jerking her head back painfully. "Hide your head in the sand for as long as you can, because before I'm through with you, you're going to be singing a different tune!"

"No—" Her whimpered protest was lost as his mouth trapped hers with devastating intent. Bracing herself to endure a punishment, she was dismayed to find his mouth softening over hers. Instead of an assault, there was tender coercion, and she began to lose the ability to think clearly.

The clean, spicy scent of the soap he used pervaded her nostrils, invading her senses. She was further weakened by the gliding smoothness of his tongue as he attempted to pry her lips apart, and she sagged weakly against him. She shivered as she felt his hand working at the knotted cord of her robe, but was powerless to stop him. The ends pulled apart, and his hand was burning the bareness of her flesh.

The gasp she uttered was her own undoing, enabling his seeking tongue to slake its hunger within the moistness of her mouth. His fingers molded the gentle swelling of her breast, arousing as well as caressing, until the pinkened tip hardened against his palm. As if this visible sign of her arousal stimulated him, his kiss became wilder, demanding and receiving a depth of response she hadn't known herself capable of until this moment.

The air chilled her dampened flesh as he moved away from her, his eyes roaming her body possessively.

"This is the image I haven't been able to forget," he groaned, his hands framing her face. "Damn you," he muttered, his words all the more shocking for having been whispered.

Staring at him with haunted eyes, Eden felt the insidious swirls of desire lifting from her numbed mind, and was appalled at how close she had come to surrendering herself. Dear God, she thought. How soon would it be before she gave in entirely, and became the walking zombie he would expect, grateful for any crumbs of affection he might care to throw her way? She had to stop him—before it was too late!

CHAPTER EIGHT

Thinking furiously, desperate to gain more time, Eden knew there was only one way she could stop this onslaught before it got completely out of hand. Every nerve in her body tensed to do what must be done, even while her mind balked at the deceit she was about to practice.

Slowly she raised her arms, placing her hands against the back of his neck, her fingers smoothing the vibrant hair at his nape with apparent enjoyment. She stood on tiptoe, allowing her nakedness to brush against his muscular body. She was being deliberately provoking, and she realized the success of her actions by the harshly increased cadence of his breathing.

"Oh, Steven," she murmured, her lips seeking and finding the rapid pulse beating in his throat. "You're right, I ache for you, but please, not tonight, not here. Dawn still occasionally has nightmares and might come to my room."

"Then we'll go to my room," he groaned, sliding his hand across the smooth flatness of her stomach in an evocative caress. Low laughter rumbled in his chest when she shivered in reaction to his roaming hand.

"She would be terrified if she found me gone, you know

that," she protested, her even, white teeth nipping playfully at his chin.

Eden felt his muscles tighten and was prepared for the moment he pulled away, lifting her chin to look suspiciously into her eyes. Keeping her face expressionless, she returned his look, although every instinct urged her to lower her lashes.

"Just what do you suggest we do?"

"Oh, I don't know." She frowned, clutching tightly at his neck in an attempt to appear frustrated. Silently uttering a little prayer, she creased her face into lines of worry. "What can we do, under the circumstances?"

His glance raked her face assessingly, and she almost gave herself away during the tense moments that followed. It took a tremendous effort on her part for her to remain still under his inspection, but finally her patience was rewarded.

Shaking his head ruefully, a slow smile curved his mouth. "You're right, little witch," he murmured, his tone regretful. "There'll be plenty of time after we're married for this kind of thing. I'll begin making arrangements tomorrow. We can leave for Reno this weekend."

"But, Steven," she protested guilelessly, careful in case he still needed further convincing. "We should do this right, for Dawn's sake. Couldn't you go see a minister in the morning, so we can be married here, with Dawn as our bridesmaid? You know how much it will mean to her."

"That will mean more of a delay than I'm prepared for," he muttered, deliberately lowering his eyes to where their bodies brushed against each other.

"I know." She sighed, laying her cheek against his chest to hide her expression. "Maybe your way is best, after all."

Just as she had hoped, her assumed deference to his

wishes had the desired effect. With a low groan he pushed her from him, his shaking hands drawing the lapels of her robe together.

"No, you're right," he said, tying the robe's cord securely. "Dawn's still so sensitive to hurt where I'm concerned that she might feel slighted if she didn't see us married."

With head bent, Eden moved past him in the direction of the door. Sensing him following, she made a supreme effort to hide the triumph she was feeling. Her hand turned the knob, opening the door quietly. Taking a deep breath, she turned to look up at him, a trembling smile on her lips.

With a moan Steven's arms came around her, and once again she knew the devastation of his kiss. By the time he released her and moved quickly from the room, she was shaking uncontrollably. Almost blindly she closed the door.

She switched off the light and turned, stumbling, into the bedroom, her shaking increasing until her teeth were chattering. She had gambled and won the time she needed to get away, but as she lay beneath the covers, the brief elation she'd felt at Steven's departure died. As she stared sightlessly out of the balcony doors at the moonglow, desolate tears formed in her eyes, and she was powerless to stop their flow from dampening her pillow.

A sleepless night left Eden with a pounding head and dark circles beneath her eyes. As she splashed cold water over her face the next morning, she looked with dissatisfaction at the puffiness of her eyelids. Even the leisurely shower she had taken hadn't done much to make her look more presentable. With a sigh she dried her skin and began rummaging in her makeup case. When in doubt, cover up. She knew with a growing sense of dread that she would probably be hiding behind her foundation lotion for a long time to come.

She checked the bathroom one last time, making sure she was leaving nothing behind. Reassured, she fastened the clasps on the makeup case, the click resounding in her head like a knell of doom. She had already stripped the sheets off the bed and remade it with fresh linen. Placing the makeup case with her other things, she then did a thorough inspection of the sitting room. She wanted to leave things in the pristine condition she had found them upon her arrival. It was a small thing to demand of herself, but somehow the cleanliness of the rooms made her feel slightly better about leaving.

She could hear the sound of running feet coming down the hall and knew the hour she dreaded had come. There was no longer any time to put off the inevitable, and her heart sank as Dawn catapulted inside.

"Eden, I . . ."

Whatever it was Dawn had been about to tell her was forever lost as the child spotted the luggage now residing in the center of the room. Eden saw confusion cross the piquant features, quickly followed by a growing dread. *Damn it!* she thought. She hadn't wanted Dawn to find out like this. She had planned on going herself to tell her she was leaving. Like the coward she knew herself to be, she had put off the heinous task until it was too late.

"Eden, w-where are you going? Do you have to leave for a while, is that it?"

"Dawn, come over here and sit down, honey," Eden said, pointing to the edge of the chaise longue. "I want to talk to you."

Agony squeezed at Eden's heart when she saw Dawn's

expression change. All animation left the endearing features, to be replaced by the familiar blankness.

"You're going away, aren't you?"

"Darling, I have to leave," she cried, walking toward the trembling child. "I don't want to leave you, but I don't have any choice. You knew I would be going home sooner or later, and, well, I just can't put it off any longer. I promise you I'll write every chance I get, and I'll send you pictures, too. I—I love you, and . . ."

"No, you don't. You don't love me," Dawn screamed, backing toward the door. "If you loved me, you wouldn't be leaving. I don't want your dumb old pictures, and if you write I—I won't e-ever write b-back."

Before she could reach her, Dawn had fled, her sobs echoing as she ran down the hallway. Brushing her hand over her eyes, Eden felt helplessness assail her. How could she leave with Dawn so upset? Turning, she looked toward her luggage. The irony of the situation struck her, and her own sobs mingled with hysterical laughter.

"You lying little . . ."

The sound of Steven's voice only barely registered before he was standing in front of Eden, his hands gripping her shoulders as he shook her unmercifully. Enduring the punishment—no, welcoming it—Eden remained silent while he vented his anger.

"What did you tell her?" he demanded, his voice harshly condemning her. "All I could make out was that you were leaving, and she never wanted to see you again."

"Oh, God, we've got to go after her," she moaned, struggling against his hold. "Please, let me go to her."

"Not until we get this mess straightened out," he muttered, flinging her away from him and raking his hand through his hair.

133

"I take it your little act of last night was just a smoke-screen," he remarked, a sneering grin curling his lips. "You never had any intention of risking the payoff, did you?"

Dully Eden looked at him, shaking her head slowly in repudiation. "You don't understand," she whispered.

"Oh, I understand all right," he retorted, his own head shaking in disgust. "You couldn't trust me to keep my promise to provide suitably for you, so you were ready to cut your losses and run, am I right?"

"That's not true," she yelled, thinking only of getting to Dawn. "I can't stand you touching me when you—"

She was going to tell him she couldn't stand being made love to by someone who despised her, but he didn't give her a chance to finish. With a savage oath he jerked her against him, and as she looked into his face, her heart almost failed her.

"Mr. Lassiter. Mr. Lassiter."

Eden almost sagged with relief when Mrs. Adams's voice reached them, accompanied by running feet.

Releasing Eden, Steven walked toward the doorway, his eyes letting her know he wasn't through with her yet.

"In here, Mrs. Adams," he called, his manner abrupt. "What is it?"

"There's a fire on the building site," she panted, standing with a hand pressed to her heaving chest. "I've called the fire department, and my Joe's down there now, trying to get it under control. Joe came running to tell me to fetch you, but he says you'd better hurry, sir."

"Dear God," he muttered, already brushing past the trembling housekeeper.

Without thinking, Eden ran after him, fear rising like bile in her throat. All she could think of was Dawn's face as she'd run from her room. *Dear God, please don't let her be in any danger,* she prayed. She had to find her, make sure she wasn't where the fire might . . .

Reaching the clearing on the shores of the lake, Eden couldn't see through the billowing smoke. She stumbled past Steven, only to be roughly hauled back by a bruising hand.

"Stay here," he yelled. Apparently changing his mind, he began pulling her with him to where James was struggling with a coiled hose, which was spewing water indiscriminately in every direction.

"Let me go," she screamed, tugging with her other hand to loosen his fingers.

"Damn it," he rasped, coughing from the smoke driven toward them on the wind. "There's too much breeze. The fire looks contained in one area, but we can't be sure it won't break out anywhere else. It's not safe to go wandering around, not until we know it's not likely to flare up under our feet."

"I don't care," she moaned, still fighting his hold. "I've got to make sure Dawn's not in there somewhere."

Steven jerked her around, taking her by the shoulders. Apparently the idea that Dawn might be in danger had never occurred to him, and now she could see the fear erupting in his streaming eyes.

"Did she say she was coming here?" he groaned, his voice anguished. "Did she?"

"It's all right, Eden," James interjected, accompanying his words by a curse when he noticed the wind changing direction.

Both she and Steven turned to him, but although Eden opened her mouth to question him, she was forestalled by Steven.

135

"You're sure she's not around here, James?"

"Positive," he smiled, nodding in the direction of Joe Adams's approaching figure. "Just ask Joe."

Joe nodded his balding head, his jaws moving steadily around the plug of chewing tobacco that was his constant solace. "Yep, I seen her running by them trees over yonder," he drawled, motioning with his head.

"The clearing." Eden breathed, looking at Steven. "She must have gone to the clearing."

Steven nodded, taking the hose from James and handing it to Eden. "You try wetting down this patch while James and I go tie into the lines on the other side of the site. You'd better come too, Joe," he yelled, already moving away.

"What if the wind changes again?" she asked, beginning the task he had given her without questioning his authority.

"If that blaze comes any closer, you get the hell out of here, is that clear?"

"Perfectly, I'm not deaf," she retorted, wrinkling her nose in the direction of his autocratic back. Turning suddenly, Steven saw the movement, and a wide grin slashed across his face, which was becoming blackened by the swirling smoke.

"We wouldn't want those freckles burnt off," he retorted, accompanying his words by a brief chuckle before moving swiftly away with Joe on his heels.

Before they were even out of sight, Eden turned her attention to the flames licking at the foundations she'd felt such pride in just the morning before. Well-seasoned wood was extremely vulnerable to fire, and the shavings from the cut wood littering the ground only added to the incendiary effect. Once alight, the wind would carry the burn-

136

ing cinders in every direction. If that happened, the blaze could be carried to the living trees, and that had to be prevented at all cost. Working mechanically, she wondered what was keeping the fire department. If this thing got any worse, they might end up with a forest fire on their hands.

As if her thoughts conjured them up, Eden heard the wailing sirens coming closer and breathed a sigh of relief. Within minutes a young, brawny fireman was relieving her of her duty, adjuring her to stay back in every bit as dictatorial a manner as Steven.

Think of the devil, she thought, watching the very essence of her thoughts walk toward her. He was almost unrecognizable, not the immaculate man she had come to know at all. His skin was smoke-blackened, the hair falling over his forehead giving him the rakish appearance of a pirate. His clothes were a mess, no longer the attractive slacks and velour shirt he'd been wearing earlier. With slashes running down both legs, and what appeared to be burn holes dotting the shirt, they were fit only for the rag bag.

"It looks like they've got everything under control," he said, a smile creasing his cheeks, leaving deep rivulets of sweat-encrusted ash in the grooves.

"Thank God," she muttered, her eyes taking in the chaotic scene around them. "Though how you can tell, I'll never understand."

"Simple enough," he admitted, nodding toward a small group of men on the edge of the clearing. "I just finished talking to the chief. I was right in thinking the fire was probably isolated, although it was difficult to tell with all the smoke. Believe it or not, the actual blaze was pretty well confined to a small area on the edge of the northern sector. Since we'd just begun building there, I think we'll find there hasn't been too much damage done."

"I'm glad," she sighed, exhaustion coloring her voice. "I would have hated to see all our hard work reduced to a pile of ashes."

Between the shock of the fire and her sleeplessness of the night before, Eden was left with a disorientation she was finding difficult to shake. Running a grubby hand over her face, she swayed, wishing she hadn't when Steven's arms came around her.

"Come on," he ordered, beginning to walk with her across the debris underfoot. "You need to get back to the house and lie down."

"No," she protested, shrugging away from his encircling arm. The frown on his face made her spirits sink even further, but she continued resolutely in the direction of the copse of trees in the distance. "I've got to find Dawn."

"The way you look you'll frighten her to death," he retorted, a derisive gleam in his eyes as he surveyed her bedraggled form. "I'll find her and send her back to the house."

"No! I've got to find her myself," she muttered, her lips pressed together firmly to stop their trembling. Strangely enough, she almost preferred Steven in his earlier mood, ranting and raving at her in an attempt to gain his own way. This kinder, more considerate man left her feeling defenseless and unable to cope with her runaway emotions.

"God, you can be a stubborn woman," he said, glaring at her in obvious frustration.

Eden didn't bother answering. They were nearing the clearing where she was sure she would find Dawn, and she increased her pace until she was nearly running. She felt annoyance at Steven's dogging pursuit, but she couldn't very well tell him to go home and leave his own child to her. If what she suspected was true, she only prayed he didn't upset Dawn further. One false move on his part toward the child could undo all the progress they'd made over the last few months, and anxiety clawed at her when she spotted the huddled figure in the middle of the clearing.

Dawn was sobbing disconsolately, deaf to their approach. Eden's heart ached with compassion when she saw the small fists clenching the spiny clumps of grass at her side. The young body was tensed, as if she were finding it difficult to contain her grief.

Dropping beside her, Eden's own eyes smarted with unshed tears as she ran a trembling hand over the child's matted hair.

"Darling, don't cry," she begged. "Everything's going to be all right."

She wasn't prepared to have Dawn turn and hurl herself into her arms, and almost reeled beneath the child's weight.

"I'm not sorry, I'm not," Dawn sobbed, her voice muffled within the warmth of Eden's throat. "Now you won't go away for a long time."

The vague suspicions Eden had been harboring blossomed into appalled certainty. "Why won't I be leaving, honey?"

"You—you s-said you were staying until those old buildings w-were finished, but I b-burned them, so you couldn't go," she screamed, beating against Eden with clenched fists. "I'm not sorry. I'm not . . ."

Ignoring the blows, Eden began rocking back and forth, hugging the hysterical little girl tighter. Raising shadowed eyes upward to where a grim-faced man stared down at them with comprehension darkening his face, Eden pleaded with her eyes. For long moments he stared into their depths, his body tensed in anger. His lips was pressed together tautly, as if he were attempting to stifle furious words, until with a muffled oath he bent and gathered his daughter into his arms.

With stumbling steps Eden followed his striding figure, listening with horror as Dawn screamed abuse at her father. His expression was grim, stony, as if he would shut out the words being thrown at him. His concentration seemed to be centered solely on getting his struggling child back to the house.

By the time they approached the front door, Dawn was quiet in Steven's arms. Mrs. Adams, her motherly face creased in concern, threw open the front door and hurried down the path to greet them.

"Let me take the little one, sir," she said.

To Eden's surprise, Steven deposited the shaking child in the housekeeper's arms.

"Take her and get her into bed, Mrs. Adams. I'm going to call the doctor, and as soon as Eden and I have cleaned up, we'll relieve you."

"Yes, Mr. Lassiter," she replied, already turning to enter the house. "The poor babe looks frightened out of her wits. Fire's a terrible thing—terrible."

"I've got to stay with her," Eden mumbled, attempting to follow Mrs. Adams's departing figure.

"First you'll do as I said," Steven demanded, grasping her arm and hauling her forward. "You can use my shower while I collect clean clothing for you. I don't want you near Dawn until you've gotten a grip on yourself."

Eden felt pain searing her with every viciously spoken

word. He was blaming her for this situation, and what made it even worse, she blamed herself. She should have found some way of breaking the news of her departure in a less shocking way for the child.

"For God's sake, don't look like that," he rasped, taking her shoulders and giving them a shake. "I didn't mean that the way it sounded. Damn it, Eden! You look like you're ready to collapse in a heap at my feet. You'll be better able to cope with Dawn after you've showered."

He didn't waste any time, she thought resentfully. Even while explaining away his rudeness, he was walking her through the brown and gold perfection of his bedroom and into the bath. Her eyes widened appreciatively when she noticed the gold accents shining from a backdrop of antique white, while her feet sank luxuriously into the deep pile of gold and white carpeting beneath her feet.

"Do you prefer a bath or a shower?" he asked. He motioned with his hand toward a sunken tub sitting in splendid isolation on a raised dais in the center of the room. He needn't have bothered pointing it out, because from almost the first moment she'd entered the bathroom, she had been unable to take her eyes from its golden oval perfection. She was seeing a new side to Steven in the splendid opulence around her, and her discoveries made her slightly uncomfortable. Although longing to immerse herself within the gleaming porcelain, her nervousness made her opt for the familiarity of the shower.

"All right," he said, his voice brisk. "You'll find towels in that cabinet over there. Here's a robe you can use until I've had a chance to collect your clothes. The hair dryer is in the third drawer of the dressing table."

"Dressing table?"

"There's a dressing room through there," he smiled,

motioning to another door leading off the bathroom. "Just exit through the dressing-room door. It leads back to my bedroom. I'm going to phone the doctor from there."

"Oh, but my clothes," she stammered, biting her lips worriedly. "It would be much better if I just used my own shower. You'll be wanting to use this one yourself."

"Are you suggesting we share this one, then?"

His voice was a mocking drawl, his eyes sparkling devilishly. Leaning one hand on the wall negligently, his glance slid from her to the large, glass-enclosed shower in the corner.

"You know I d-didn't mean anything of the kind," she mumbled, avoiding his eyes. "I just thought you'd prefer using your own shower, that's all."

As if tired of baiting her, he straightened, his face becoming once again a sardonic mask. "Don't worry," he snapped. "I'll be using the bathroom off my study. I suggest you hurry. The doctor won't take long to arrive. Since I assume you'd like to talk to Dawn before he gets here, I wouldn't waste any time if I were you. I want him to give her something to help her sleep."

"Yes, yes, of course."

Steven only nodded, and when he left her to follow his orders, the room felt strangely empty. She looked around her for a moment, until thoughts of the unhappy child occupying the farthest wing of this vast house had her scurrying to discard her ruined clothing.

Eden had to admit that she felt much better after her shower. Shrugging into the clean-smelling robe Steven had provided, she walked into the dressing room, smiling when she repeatedly tripped over the trailing ends of the masculine terry-cloth covering. She found the blow dryer in the exact spot he had said she would, but that didn't surprise her. She would be amazed if the arrogant Steven Lassiter was ever wrong about anything!

As soon as her hair was partially dry, Eden returned the dryer to its proper drawer. She hoped he wouldn't mind her using his comb, but if he did, that was just too bad. He hadn't thought to provide her with her own, and she derived great satisfaction over the simple omission. It proved he wasn't as perfect as he thought, she mused childishly.

After tidying the bathroom and adjacent dressing room, Eden timidly entered Steven's bedroom. She breathed a sigh of relief on finding it empty, her eyes going at once to the clothes spread on the bed. She flushed when she thought of him handling her things, especially when her gaze took in the lacy bra and panties lying beside her green jersey dress.

With as much speed as possible she slipped into her clothing, her eyes going toward the closed door every few moments. She felt foolish when it remained closed, and her cheeks heated as she bent to fasten the white sandals on her bare feet. Steven had forgotten to provide nylons, and the bareness of her tanned legs made her feel curiously vulnerable. *Another slip-up, Mr. Lassiter!* she thought.

Entering Dawn's room, she smiled as Mrs. Adams approached. "How is she?"

"I don't know!" Mrs. Adams's pleasant face was creased in worry. "She seems to be shutting things out the way she used to. Could she be suffering from shock?"

Assuming a confidence she was far from feeling to reassure the worried woman, Eden said, "She'll be all right. Steven's calling the doctor. If it is shock, she'll be treated for it."

"Well, I'm just glad you're here. Poor baby's been calling for you."

Eden flinched, her eyes going to the huddled figure beneath the covers of the pretty French provincial canopy with its autumn leaf design. Steven had gone to great trouble in designing a room his daughter would be comfortable in, she thought. Although she had spent many hours here with Dawn, she had never taken the room's beauty for granted. The white and gold furniture was perfect for a little girl, but it was the woodsy mural that caught the eye. The walls had been hand-painted to represent a forest, with endearing animals peeping through the foliage. The carpet was as soft as the green moss covering a forest glade, the ceiling the light blue of a summer day. This room reflected the love and concern Steven had for his child, and Eden's heart ached with pity when she remembered his face as he carried a vitriolic Dawn in his arms, his expression forgiving as he endured the pain her words must have caused him.

"Eden . . . Eden . . ."

"Yes, darling," she murmured, rushing over to sit on the edge of the bed. "I'm here, sweetheart."

"Promise you won't leave me, promise," Dawn begged, her little hand groping for Eden's reassuring clasp.

Carrying the small hand to her lips, Eden closed her eyes.

"I promise," she murmured, her lips moving stiffly against the child's skin.

"I—I'm sorry about the fire," she mumbled, her head flailing from side to side while tears poured silently from her remorseful eyes. "You were going away, and I h-had to stop you. I didn't mean to be b-bad. You don't hate me, do you?"

"I could never hate you," Eden gasped, gathering the distraught child against her. "You're as much a part of me as if you were my own little girl, and I'll always love you, always."

Snuggling her head against Eden's breast, Dawn's thin arms wandered up to clasp her neck tightly.

"You'll never leave me?"

"Never in this life, sweetheart!"

A slight sound from the doorway attracted Eden's attention. Steven stood there with another man she presumed to be the doctor. As they entered, she seemed incapable of tearing her gaze from him. He was strangely forbidding as he halted by the foot of the bed, but when she saw the glittering triumph reflected in his eyes, she understood. A silent message passed between them. When a sardonic grin slashed his face, Eden shivered.

CHAPTER NINE

Eden didn't feel married. In fact, she made it a practice
to feel very little at all. If the situation between her and
Steven wasn't the richly rewarding time of discovery everyone supposed, she tried not to let it bother her. Their
relationship was at a stalemate, with Steven spending as
much time as possible away from the house. The only
times they were together, either Dawn or James were
present—and Eden intended keeping it that way.

She had left Steven in no doubt that she wouldn't tolerate any attempts at lovemaking, and so far he had respect-
ed her wishes. After the brief ceremony conducted by the
local pastor in a flower-decked living room, Eden had
circulated among their guests with a smile, until she felt
her face would crack. Dawn had been her only consolation
on that day, she remembered. Adorable in pink and white
chiffon, she had taken her role as bridesmaid seriously,
afterward catering to the needs of their neighbors with
remarkable self-assurance for such a shy child.

That she was happy was obvious. Every few minutes she
would return to Eden, her feet skipping across the floor in
the white patent leather shoes which were her pride. Stev-
en had invited her friend from school, the fashionable
Mary Ann, and Dawn was having a wonderful time acting

the grand lady. That Mary Ann was suitably impressed was very obvious. She followed Dawn with worshipful eyes, and Eden was overjoyed to notice how often the two heads were bent toward each other, their giggles causing amused stares in their direction. At last Dawn was discovering what it was to belong.

The opposite could be said for me, she thought. She knew Steven still desired her. At times she could see raw desire flare in his eyes, but those times were happening less and less. He avoided her now, almost as though he were waiting for her to come to him. Well, he would turn old and gray before she would swallow her pride to that extent. She knew he thought it was only a matter of time before her own desires overcame her resistance, but she didn't care what he thought.

Of course, they hadn't bothered with a honeymoon. With the cleanup after the fire increasing the need for supervision on the building site, no one was surprised when they remained at home. For that Eden was thankful. She didn't want anyone speculating about the success of her marriage, although with Steven becoming even more bad-tempered as the weeks passed, it wouldn't be long before people guessed that theirs wasn't a marriage made in heaven.

With a sigh Eden packed the last of Dawn's outgrown clothing in a box, ready to be delivered to the bazaar that weekend. Mrs. Adams would be running the used-clothing stall, and the money would go toward helping to fund a badly needed day-care center for working mothers. Dawn would be spending the day at the bazaar with Mary Ann and her parents, and returning with Mary Ann for a much-longed-for pajama party Saturday night. Several other little girls from Dawn's class were invited, and

Dawn had been in a state of nervous excitement all week. On several occasions, Eden had been forced to speak sharply to her, something Dawn was beginning to need with satisfactory regularity. Her natural ebullience, too long repressed, was coming to the fore with a vengeance, Eden thought with a smile, as she fastened the lid on the box.

"Mom, where are you?"

"In here, darling," Eden called, her mouth quirking at Dawn's enthusiastic entrance. Sometimes it seemed as if the word *walk* had been dropped from her vocabulary.

"Guess what? We're going on a field trip tomorrow to the caverns, and the bus has broken down!"

Dusting her hands together, Eden stood, an inquiring tilt to one finely shaped brow as she faced the grinning child.

"I know," she smiled. "I signed the permission slip, remember?"

"Oh, yeah. I forgot!"

"I thought you were looking forward to the trip," Eden remarked, pushing the box into the closet with Dawn's help. "Why so delighted that the bus has broken down?"

"Because now the parents get to take us—look!"

With a wry twist to her lips Eden took the proferred piece of paper, well-creased from its stay in Dawn's back pocket. Smoothing it out, she saw that it was a request for parents willing to drive, and she looked toward Dawn with mock ferociousness.

"Just what makes you so sure I'd even want to take a bunch of screaming kids on a field trip, young lady?"

Dawn hugged Eden's waist, a small giggle escaping her. "Oh, Mom," she chortled. "Don't be dumb. You know you want to go."

"Oh, I do, do I?"

Suddenly doubtful, Dawn looked up, a frown replacing her earlier eagerness. "You will go, won't you? I'll like it much better if you're there. Please?"

"Young lady, you're getting to be extremely spoiled. Has anyone told you that?"

"Just you!"

"You're also learning to bat your eyelashes quite effectively. Whom have you been practicing on?" she laughed, leading Dawn out of the room with a casual arm slung across her shoulders. "Not that boy in your class that you and Mary Ann were raving about when she spent the night last weekend, by any chance?"

A flush colored Dawn's cheeks as she glanced guiltily in Eden's direction. "He is kinda cute," she admitted, an unrepentant grin curving her mouth.

"You'd better not let Daddy hear you talking about your boyfriends," she warned, her eyes twinkling. "He thinks he's the only man in your life."

"I know," she sighed in satisfaction. "You know how fathers are. They just won't admit you're grown up."

Eden laughed, her arm tightening around Dawn in a fierce hug. As Steven had promised, he had arranged for several future commissions from people needing the services of an architect, enough to keep Eden busy for quite a long time to come. Although satisfied career-wise, she couldn't help but feel her greatest happiness came from this wonderful new closeness between Steven and Dawn. At least that much good had been achieved by their marriage!

"Well, I guess we'd better go and call your teacher. If I'm going to drive tomorrow, I'll need the directions."

"I knew you'd do it," Dawn crowed, jumping about and nearly tripping Eden in the process. "You're going to love it," Dawn chortled, her eyes dancing.

By the time she returned home the next day from the outing with Dawn's class, Eden was aching in muscles she hadn't even known she possessed. A shower helped to relieve some of the soreness, but didn't do much to alleviate the restlessness that assailed her when Mrs. Adams greeted her with the news that Steven wouldn't be back until late.

He's impossible! she raged silently, remembering the curious glance that had colored Mrs. Adams's expression. Maintaining a cool composure she was far from feeling, she had given the woman the night off, unable to bear the idea of spending the evening fending off another barrage of seemingly innocent questions. The only concession to married status they had made were adjoining bedrooms, but Eden was beginning to suspect that Mrs. Adams wasn't a bit fooled by the arrangement.

Sliding a lemon and brown caftan over her head, she stepped into low-heeled brown mules. After giving her hair a desultory combing, she threw down the brush with disgust. Brown eyes, dulled with despairing loneliness, surveyed her surroundings. A strawberry botanical print hung at the windows, while the fabric covering the slipper chair in the corner was of stemmed cherries on a cool white background. Keeping with the vineyard theme, the chaise in the center of the large room sported tiny leafed strawberries, while the bed became the focal point, with rushed satin pillows and appliquéd quilt.

It was a lovely warm room, the rosewood dresser and

mirrored dressing table glowing with the patina of age, but Eden took no pleasure in it. She felt a fraud, and turned to look at the locked communicating door into Steven's room with a glare of dislike. Suddenly she longed for the functional familiarity of her apartment in Los Angeles, remembering how often she had felt trapped within its small rooms. With a wry twist to her mobile lips, she wondered if she was always to go through life looking behind her.

She wished now that she hadn't agreed to Dawn spending an extra night with Mary Ann, but when Mary Ann's mother had explained that it would enable them to get an earlier start for the bazaar in the morning, she couldn't very well refuse. She had assured Eden that clothes were no problem, the girls being much the same size, and so she had driven home alone with this quite illogical sense of depression nagging at her.

If there had been time, she had hoped to spend the rest of the afternoon with Dawn. She thought they might have toured Shasta Dam, which had created the beauty of Shasta Lake, or possibly the old town of Shasta, if Dawn would like that better. They had once gone with James, but there hadn't been nearly enough time to absorb the atmosphere of what had once been a thriving Old-West community. The advent of the railroad had left it a virtual ghost town, but although what had been the main street was now little more than rubble marking where the buildings had stood, there was still a fascinating old museum located in the building that used to be the courthouse.

With an exclamation of disgust, Eden left her room. There wasn't any use in brooding over what might have been. The only thing that would put an end to this restlessness was work, she thought, heading for the screened porch at the back of the house which she had converted into an office. Once there, she automatically headed for the large drafting table that was covered by the drawings she had made of the completed project. Almost immediately she became absorbed, staring at the colorful plans with a vague feeling of dissatisfaction.

Something about the proposed completion of the resort was bothering her. For the last week she had felt as if there was something obvious she had forgotten to consider. Biting her lip, she studied the minute details as she had so many times before, but there still remained a sensation of uncertainty. With a sigh she stood back, rubbing the back of her neck absentmindedly. Vague ideas formed in her mind and were almost immediately discarded. Her attention wandered to the shaded area denoting the lake's perimeter. Her imagination blossomed with thoughts of the pleasure to be found within the cool depths of the water. She remembered with a tingle of envy the sight of the many varied crafts skimming the distant surface. She could spend all her time upon the water and luxuriate in the indolence of every sun-filled day. In fact, many tourists did just that, renting houseboats and traveling from one part of the lake to another. Often whole families . . .

Houseboats . . . families . . . That's it! A growing excitement clutched her. Grabbing a pencil, she began sketching feverishly, losing all sense of time as her ideas began to flow from her brain to her hand. Hour after hour passed unheeded, until the increasing dimness of early evening put a stop to her labor. Stretching her back with a groan, a satisfied smile curved her lips as she surveyed her plans. She wondered why she hadn't thought of it before—the one thing that would make their resort on the shores of the lake unique. She couldn't think of anything more calculated to draw tourists than a central entertainment center catering to their children, with trained instructors in water safety and wilderness survival instead of just licensed baby-sitters. Parents would be free to relax with other adults, knowing their offspring were not only being well cared for, but also were having fun geared to appeal to them.

Renters of houseboats would also be included, with docking facilities in the special area she had just designed. They could enjoy the dining and shopping facilities of the resort while at the same time their children could revel in a lack of confinement for several hours.

Glancing at her watch, she realized it was time to prepare dinner, although she was too stimulated to be very hungry. Hurrying toward the kitchen, suppressed excitement lent speed to her steps. Her earlier depression was forgotten beneath an aura of achievement, and she hummed softly to herself as her hands deftly shredded lettuce for a salad.

"Is that all you're prepared to feed a starving man?"

"James, when did you get back?"

Turning to greet the smiling man entering the kitchen, she noted his air of restrained satisfaction with a grin.

"I take it your visit was successful," she teased, wiping her hands on a towel before reaching for the crystal wineglasses in the upper cupboard.

"Here, let me get those for you," he offered, suiting action to words. "Are we celebrating something?"

"Yes," she said, wrinkling her nose, "but I'm not going to be the first one to give any glad news. Did you ask her?"

James had been gone the last few days, hiring extra builders for the project, but only Eden knew he had been combining business with pleasure. While in Sacramento he had been staying with the family of the girl he was in love with, and he had confided his intention of asking her to marry him. She remembered how nervous he had been just discussing it, and now her face crinkled in laugh lines as she waited for his answer.

"You're finding all of this so amusing, I shouldn't even tell you," he retorted, following her into the dining room.

"You wouldn't dare," she muttered threateningly, setting the table with deceptively calm movements. He smiled, his expression innocent. With the intention of punishing him for his irritating teasing, she stopped him when he was about to speak, motioning him to a chair with a casual wave of her hand.

"Go ahead and start on your salad while I go and put a steak under the broiler."

Without giving him the time to protest, she reentered the kitchen, her shoulders shaking with amusement. He had looked like a fish, his mouth opening and closing disconcertedly at her assumed lack of curiosity, but it served him right, she thought. Her eyes twinkling, she unwrapped a frozen steak and placed it in the microwave to defrost.

A few minutes later she withdrew the steak and placed it under the broiler. By the time she had reset the serving tray with appropriate cutlery, a tantalizing aroma of sizzling beef teased her nostrils, and she almost wished she had prepared one for herself. Too late now, she thought regretfully. If she didn't get back in there, James was going to burst. He loved to drag every last ounce of drama out of any situation, and her willingness to put off hearing his news must be killing him.

Placing his meal in front of him, she ignored his reproachful glare, seating herself calmly beside him with a carefree smile.

"I hope it's rare enough for you," she said, keeping her face composed with a great deal of effort.

She knew he was waiting for her to question him again by his recurring glances in her direction as she calmly lifted a bite of salad to her mouth. Chewing with every evidence of enjoyment, she ignored the thunderous frown on his brow, at last glancing at him in innocent inquiry.

"Is there something the matter with your steak?"

"Damn the steak," he muttered, shaking his head in hurt reproach. "Don't you even care whether or not Susan said yes?"

Unable to contain her laughter any longer, her voice rose in delighted peals of mirth. For a moment James looked startled, until his eyes encountered the teasing affection in Eden's. Soon they were both enjoying the situation, their hilarity easing when James gave a wry shake of his head.

"I deserved that, didn't I?"

"You certainly did," she grinned. "You don't know how long I've waited for the opportunity to give you a taste of your own medicine," she admitted.

"Well, you certainly kept me hanging that time!"

Silence prevailed while he happily cut into his meat and began to eat it. He chewed contentedly until finally Eden sighed in exasperation.

"James, if you don't tell me whether or not you're going to become a married man, I'm going to wring your neck!"

Jumping up, much to Eden's annoyance, James left the room. Really, she thought, staring frustratedly at the doorway through which he disappeared. He must be the most irresponsible, annoying . . . The flow of her mental recriminations stopped when James reappeared, an open bottle of wine in his hand. She watched in silence as he carefully poured the rich burgundy liquid into their glasses, determined not to give him the satisfaction of seeing her eagerness. Once more seating himself, he raised his glass aloft, his eyes sparkling devilishly as they gazed into hers.

"Here's to my future wife," he remarked casually.

"I knew it," she squealed, jumping up and throwing her arms around his neck. "Oh, James, you infuriating darling. I'm so happy I could cry."

Caught up in the excitement of the moment, neither were aware of another presence, until a drawling voice spoke from the hallway.

"Is all that affection for James, or do you have a little left over for your husband?"

"Steven," she whispered. Straightening, Eden clutched the back of James's chair, her face flushing as she met the derision in his eyes. "Mrs. Adams told me you wouldn't be home for dinner."

"She was right," he said, his manner abrupt.

"I w-was just going to get some coffee," she stammered. "Sit down and I'll get you a cup."

When she returned with the coffee, Steven and James were deep in discussion. Pouring the steaming beverage, she studied Steven from beneath her lashes, flushing in confusion when he looked up suddenly and caught her staring at him.

"I—I'll just clean up here," she murmured, her movements fidgety. She hoped fervently that he wouldn't notice her clumsiness. Although James was blithely unaware of it, Eden could tell Steven was angry—furiously angry. It was there in the tautness of his muscular frame and in the whiteness around his compressed lips. Carrying the dishes into the kitchen, she was glad to escape his oppressive presence, her hands shaking as she loaded the dishwasher.

"Where's Steven?" Eden unconsciously frowned as she questioned James. She had mentally braced herself to return to the dining room, only to find James alone, contentedly finishing his meal.

Steven's chair reproached her by its very emptiness, and it suddenly seemed to be the last straw. She had tried so hard to appear uncaring when he went out of his way to avoid her, but damn it! It hurt! He hadn't wanted a wife in the truest sense of the word, but that didn't mean she would stand for being treated like part of the furniture. Glaring at James as if he were somehow responsible, she repeated her question.

"Hey," he murmured, his eyes upset. "Is there something I missed?"

"I—I'm sorry," she stammered, her earlier anger dissipating into a tight ball of misery. Attempting to hide her churning emotions, she forced a laugh from between trembling lips, but it must have sounded as shaky as it felt, because James studied her in rising awareness.

"What's the matter, honey?"

"Don't be silly," she murmured, avoiding his too perceptive gaze. "I—I've got a headache, that's all. I really shouldn't drink wine when I know it doesn't agree with me."

James's expression registered his disbelief; his eyes went from her still-full glass to her face in one fluid motion. She smiled brightly in an attempt to allay his suspicions.

"Let's go outside," she suggested, and to her relief he followed quietly, sensing her need for a change of subject. Once outside, Eden walked restlessly toward the gazebo marking the entrance to the garden. Gratefully she breathed in the sultry fragrance of the night-blooming flowers. A gentle breeze lifted her hair, carrying the ever-present scent of pine trees in its wake.

James didn't follow immediately, and she was grateful. That was the nice thing about James, she thought. He always seemed to look beneath the surface of things, understanding her needs before she was even aware of them herself. Why couldn't she have fallen in love with someone like him? A sigh accompanied the silent question, and she raised her head to stare into the mysterious night sky, as if the myriad stars glittering brightly could give her the answer. As the moments passed, she felt a sensation of peace enfolding her. The velvet softness of the night wove its magic, calming her as nothing else could. When she heard James's approaching footsteps, she was once again fully in control of her emotions, and she turned toward him almost eagerly.

"I don't know how I can bear to shut myself up in the office for most of the day," she confessed, shaking her head. "There's so much beauty here, so much visual wealth to be plundered, it seems a shame to miss a moment of it."

"I know what you mean," he agreed, his own gaze trying to pierce the ever-increasing shadows. "You must be glad that the planning stage is over and approved. You've done a splendid job, Eden. Steven's a difficult man to please, but he was singing your praises the other day."

James wasn't fooling her a bit! He knew something was wrong between her and Steven, and this was his way of trying to make things a little better. She couldn't imagine Steven admitting, to James or anyone else, that she was good for anything. Still, she wasn't about to argue the matter. She wouldn't waste another moment in vain regrets, but would instead try to recapture her earlier satisfaction in the changes she had planned.

She began telling him her ideas, leaning against the natural wood railing of the arched gazebo. As she talked, her face lighted up enthusiastically, with her hands punctuating her words as her excitement increased.

To her delight the ever-ebullient James grabbed her around the waist in a bear hug that threatened to crack her ribs.

"You brilliant sweetheart," he enthused, swinging her feet off the floor. She was gasping for breath, her laughter ringing on the night air like twinkling chimes, her hands locked together behind his neck. "Steven's going to . . ."

"Steven's going to what, old buddy?"

Her own gasp was almost choked off completely by the bone-crushing tightening of James's arms. Slowly she was lowered until her slippered feet touched smooth wooden planks. Steven's voice dripped venom, and she saw the shock registering on James's face. It was there in the frozen stillness of his expression and the tenseness of his body keeping his arms locked convulsively around her waist.

"Hey, man, you've got this all wrong!"

"The only thing I got wrong was trusting you to keep your damn hands off my wife," he snarled, approaching the gazebo with leashed fury.

James's muscles tensed for a brief moment before he released Eden and turned to face Steven, his usually good-natured countenance now reflecting a steadily building anger of his own. Until she came, the two had been the best of friends and now here they were, facing each other

160

like vicious enemies. She had to stop this before it got out of hand, before irreparable damage was done to a valued relationship.

"You don't understand anything if you think James low enough to flirt with me behind your back," she whispered, her eyes wide in her pale face as she looked at Steven. "Don't jump to disgusting conclusions. James can explain . . ."

"The only thing James is going to do is get the hell out of here," he snapped, his narrow-eyed glance piercing her with baleful intensity. "Now!"

"Like hell I will, with you in this mood," James interjected, moving closer to Eden in a protective gesture. "I'm not leaving her to try to explain anything to you. You treat her like the dirt under your feet as it is. I wouldn't put it past you to do worse."

"Are you accusing me of abusing my wife?"

Eden closed her eyes at the dangerously muted tone of Steven's voice. She knew the signs of his anger too well and suddenly realized it wouldn't take much more to send him over the edge of reasonable behavior. She was frightened, more frightened by the possible outcome of this confrontation between the two men than by any threat to herself. Somehow she knew instinctively that no matter how enraged he was with her, Steven wouldn't enact the kind of physical punishment James envisioned. No! she remembered, her stomach muscles tightening sickeningly. He had subtler, more devastating ways of relaying his displeasure.

"There are all kinds of abuse," James retorted, his eyes sparkling dangerously. "For God's sake, man! Eden's a wife any man would be proud of. Yet when she's not slaving away on this damn project you're so obsessed with,

161

or taking care of your daughter, she's wandering around the house without your giving a damn that she's lonely."

"Is that what you're trying to do?" Steven sneered. "Alleviate some of her loneliness?"

"Somebody should try, since you sure as hell don't!"

Eden had taken all she could stand. Being caught in what appeared to be a compromising situation was one thing, but pity was another. Without stopping to think, she stamped her foot, her hands clutching the bones of her hips furiously.

"All right," she stormed, her head swiveling back and forth between the two astounded men. "If the two of you want to take your frustrations out on each other, be my guest. It doesn't matter a tinker's damn to me what you do. Kill yourselves for all I care, only I'm not staying around to watch!"

"Eden, I . . ."

The concern in James's voice was almost her undoing, and she had to struggle to contain her tears as she paused to glance at him.

"James, you're a wonderful friend, but I don't need you or anyone else to fight my battles for me. If you want to show me you care for me, then leave, please!"

To her relief James, after studying her taut expression for brief seconds, did as she asked, but not before leveling a last parting shot at Steven which left Eden wincing in dismay.

"I've always admired you, old buddy, but if you can't see what's right in front of your face, then you haven't got the intelligence of a jackass!"

There was a lot to be said for dropping dead, and at this moment Eden could think of a hundred good reasons to cease her present existence. Tears of humiliation ran down her cheeks as the enormity of the situation struck her. Raising appalled eyes to Steven's face, she noticed the incredulity of his expression with anguish. She couldn't stand it if James's words caused him to suspect the truth she had barely acknowledged to herself, and with a muffled sob she backed away from his still figure, shaking her head.

"Eden, look out!"

His cry of warning came too late, and Eden felt herself hurtling backward down the gazebo steps. She saw Steven throw himself forward in an attempt to catch her flailing hand, his large figure assuming nightmarish proportions against the steadily dimming light. A piercing pain enveloped her head, and her groan was almost a cry of relief as she gave herself up to comforting darkness.

CHAPTER TEN

Her unconsciousness couldn't have lasted more than a few minutes, because when she opened her eyes, she was still lying at the bottom of the steps. The only difference was that now she was partially supported by Steven's muscular frame.

"Are you all right?"

She didn't even try to kid herself into believing that the concern in his voice was sincere. Jerkily she pulled away from his supporting arms, wincing as a brief pain sliced through her temple.

"I'm fine," she muttered, her trembling fingers feeling the bruised spot on the back of her head. "Are you afraid James will think you pushed me?"

His scathing retort was appropriate for the viciousness of the accusation, and Eden didn't even bother to defend herself. She couldn't believe she had thought the words, let alone spoken them. She was just about ready to utter a shamed apology when she was lifted high against his chest. The warmth of his body penetrated the fine cambric of his shirt, and she struggled ineffectively to escape his closeness.

"Let me go," she demanded, her alarm growing in proportion to his distance-eating stride. Silently he carried her across the patio and into the house. A quick glance upward was all she needed to convince her that his anger hadn't abated one bit. He looked murderous!

"Steven, please . . . I . . ."

"Shut up!"

Eden bit her lip to keep from crying aloud as he passed the door to her bedroom without altering his stride. She thought he surely must be able to feel the pounding of her heart, so fiercely did the beat accelerate. Her breath was coming in fitful gasps when he threw open the door and entered the shadowed interior of his bedroom, shutting it firmly by levering his back against it.

"Put me down!"

For a breathless second he hesitated, his brooding gaze intent on her frightened face. Her eyes scanned the mercilessness of his features, but all hope for a reprieve fled when his head shook slowly.

"You can't do this," she whispered.

"You're my wife!"

The words reverberated in her brain with a force that left her shaken. As if her last restraint had snapped, she struggled for release, her head flailing wildly from side to side. Her fists beating against his hard chest had little effect, and her frantic protests fell on deaf ears as he dumped her unceremoniously upon his massive bed.

"That's a laugh," she taunted, already beyond the bonds of rational thinking. "James was right, you—"

"Unless you want to send me completely around the bend, don't mention his name. Not now!"

Scrambling upright on her knees, she watched his hands slowly work at the buttons of his shirt. In horror she saw him slide the garment carelessly from his shoulders. In unwilling fascination her eyes moved from the rippling strength of his shoulders to his chest. The softly curling hairs in the center captured her gaze, her eyes automatically traveling downward to where the narrowing line disappeared into the waistband of his black slacks.

"You won't think it's so amusing in a little while," he promised, his eyes glittering with arousal. "After tonight James won't be able to accuse me of neglecting you!"

"You animal," she hissed, moving backward across the bed. "What are you going to do, brag to him about how you raped your own wife?"

A slow smile softened the rigidity of his mouth, but far from reassuring her, she felt even more disoriented than before.

"I won't have to tell him anything," he murmured, his hands going to the waistband of his trousers. "By tomorrow I'll have made you my woman so thoroughly that James won't be able to close his eyes to the reality of my possession, and neither will you, my conniving, lonely little wife. I've taken about all I can stand of the reproach in those chocolate eyes of yours. Now you're going to get what you've been asking for, and believe me, honey, it won't be rape!"

Time was running out for Eden. As if he were tired of baiting her, he quickly and unashamedly divested himself of the remainder of his clothing. With a muffled groan, she flung herself backward toward the opposite side of the bed, her hopeful eyes alighting on the bedroom door.

Hope flared briefly and then died when she felt a large hand grasp her ankle, dragging her back to the center of the bed. Her hands clutched frantically at the softness of the fur spread to gain leverage, but to no avail. The indignity of her position brought a recurrence of the tears she'd shed earlier. Her caftan had ridden up above her waist, baring her underwear, and she pounded her clenched fists helplessly against the softness of the bed.

"Mmmm, I've not had the pleasure of this view before," he murmured, a low laugh rumbling in his chest.

Before she could reach down to cover herself, she felt a warm, melting sensation at the base of her spine, and her eyes opened wide with shock when she realized the cause. His mouth was moving softly over the dimpled indentation, leaving a burning trail of sensation implanted on her sensitive flesh as it traveled to the scanty covering afforded by her bikini panties. Without raising his mouth from her soft skin, his hands curved over the bones of her slim hips, his thumbs levering the minuscule lace covering to bare new territory for his roaming lips to discover. A groan forced itself from deep in his throat, the warmth of his breath increasing the ever-growing arousal knotting her stomach with incredible yearning. Although hardly audible, the sound was enough to jerk her out of the sensuous daze she had fallen into.

"Don't! Oh, please, not like this!"

Her pleading fell on deaf ears, her struggles only serving to facilitate his movements as he stripped her of the flimsy barrier. Pivoting onto her back with one knee raised, she attempted to kick out at him, only to find her legs trapped easily by his muscular thigh. Her fingers formed claws intent on marring the smoothness of his skin, but even that was denied her when they were grasped easily and lifted over her head by one ample hand. His other moved to the zipper of her caftan, moving it downward in one swift, sure motion. Her head was arched back in an attempt to avoid his descending mouth, but he only used the opportunity to enjoy the distended pulse points of her throat.

"Don't fight me," he muttered, his lips moving feverishly against her neck and shoulders. "Dear God, I want you!"

Want—not love! The words seared her mind, bringing an agonizing misery in their wake. Already her body was the betrayer, her smooth flesh softening under the coaxing warmth of his hand. To be taken like this because of a basic need any woman could fulfill was to Eden the depths of degradation, made even more unbearable by her own love for this dour, taciturn man she'd married. He would strip everything from her. She knew that as surely as she knew she drew in breath. He would leave her with no self-respect, taking but never giving her what she really craved. Eventually she wouldn't be able to resist giving him her body to use. In truth, she was nearly at that point now. She was a prisoner of her own emotions, forced to walk forever in the painful twilight of a love he'd never sought . . . and would never welcome.

She didn't stop fighting him because he had demanded it of her, but because she could no longer resist giving the only thing she could give openly and freely—her body. He hadn't asked for her love, which she would have presented to him with searing joy. No, he only asked for her flesh, the outward trappings of her soul, but if it was the only part of her he wanted, then so be it! He would never know or care that he was being cheated, but even as she raised her arms to his neck in a gesture almost of supplication, slow tears poured from beneath tightly shut eyes. She knew, and, dear God, how she cared!

His mouth moved gently over her eyelids, his lips and tongue drinking the saltiness of her pain with sensitive deliberation.

"Look at me, Eden!"

Slowly her eyes opened, his demand making it impossible for her to continue hiding in the darkness. The light still shining from the patio illuminated his features; his eyes glowed with slumbrous passion as they locked with hers. The breath caught in her throat from the intensity of his stare. He seemed to be trying to tell her something without words, but she was only conscious of the sheer male beauty of him. He was like a brooding pagan god as he leaned over her, the light catching his amber hair and turning it into an aureole of living fire.

She thought she was prepared for a continuance of his lovemaking, but when his hand moved to part her thighs, she flinched, her body tightening in silent protest. His eyes narrowed furiously at the movement, as well as at the unspoken reproach in her eyes. When he rolled away from her with a disgusted groan, she wasn't prepared for the action. Sitting bolt upright, she stared in disbelief at the taut muscles of his back as he lay facedown on the bed.

"S-Steven, I . . ."

"Get out!"

The harsh words were accompanied by a string of expletives as his hands, in a cruel mockery of her earlier struggles, clutched the spread until the knuckles showed white. When she stayed immobile in frozen silence, his muffled taunt seared into her flesh, piercing her heart until she felt as if she were bleeding inside.

"The last thing I need is an unwilling woman," he said, turning his head to rake her with hostile eyes. "James is welcome to you!"

Gathering together the trailing ends of her clothing, she scrambled to her feet, pain going too deep to find expression in her features. With the tattered remains of her shattered pride, she turned, walking from the man she loved so desperately, and she felt as if a part of herself were being ripped away.

Even though he hadn't bothered to complete the lesson, Steven had achieved one thing he had set out to do. It was there in James's eyes when he entered her office the next morning. She nearly cringed beneath the intensity of his look and his eyes widened in sympathetic understanding. Their clear blue reflected the mark of Steven's possession as they fastened on the small bruise at the side of her throat, and she quickly buttoned her white jersey blouse to her neck with shaking hands.

"Are you all right?"

Her smile was just a brief flutter of her lips before she turned back to her work.

"Of course," she replied, trying to avoid further discussion by injecting a note of cool disdain into her voice.

"Where's Steven?"

"How should I know?" she answered, accompanying her words with an uncaring shrug of her shoulders.

"Damn it, Eden! If he hurt you I'll . . ."

"He didn't hurt me," she remarked, an unamused laugh startling her by its harshness. "Not in the way you mean it, at least."

"No, but I'm not a fool," he retorted, refusing to let the matter drop. "I can guess at his methods!"

"Just stay out of it, James," she said tiredly, shaking her head and staring unseeingly at the drawing in front of her. "The way his mind is working regarding the two of us, Steven wouldn't listen to a thing you had to say. If you try to interfere, it'll only make things worse than they already are."

"If you think I'm going to stand meekly to the side and watch him destroy you, you'd better think again, Eden."

Really alarmed now, she turned beseeching eyes in his direction.

"James, promise me you won't—" she began, only to be abruptly silenced by the slashing movement of his arm.

"Like hell!"

Eden gazed after his departing figure with distraught eyes. The mood he was in could have disastrous results if he were to meet up with Steven. Neither of the men were in the sweetest of tempers at the moment. With a sigh, she faced the inevitability of another meeting between the two. It was just one more thing to worry about, and her head was aching as it was. What little sleep she'd managed the night before had been riddled with nightmares as she relived the devastating emotions of her encounter with Steven. She realized how perfidious dreams could be the moment she opened her eyes. In her reveries Steven hadn't sent her away! Shame coursed through her anew as she recalled the early morning sunlight bathing her perspiring flesh, her body languid with the haunting fulfillment of her dreams.

Dropping her pencil with a clatter, she rose to her feet, pushing her hand back from her brow. She had to get out of here, and quickly. Perhaps by hiding in the tall grass of the quiet forest glade she could recapture her objectivity, she thought, already heading for the back exit of the screened porch. If not, at least the cool breezes from the shade trees might restore a little of the calm she so sadly lacked. Either way, she needed to escape from this house that exuded Steven's presence before she made a complete fool of herself.

The glade worked its magic, and Eden felt her nervousness dissipating on the wind. It wasn't nearly as hot as it had been the day before; the harsh glare of the sun was blanketed by gray and white clouds skudding across the gentle blue skies. Lying back, she played a game she hadn't thought of since childhood—that of trying to depict shapes in the billowy puffs.

Eden didn't know what it was that awakened her. One moment she was at peace, her body revitalizing itself with healing sleep, and the next her eyes were opened, staring across the glade with cold fear clutching her heart.

Steven stood, proud and straight in the distance, a gun raised to his shoulder. It was worse than a nightmare. She saw the barrel of the gun pointing at the center of the glade where a young deer stood poised, ears twitching alertly in uneasiness.

She wanted to scream, but no sound could get past the tight ball of misery lodging in her throat. Beside the nearly full-grown male was a female, her hind quarters dragging pathetically behind her as she moved to crop the grass. She must have managed a strangled moan, because the male leaped forward, disappearing behind the shelter of the surrounding trees. But the female, the poor, crippled female . . .

It was almost as if she were watching a slow motion segment on television, but this was real, horrifyingly real. A sharp report rent the stillness, and with a sobbing moan Eden watched the stricken animal fall, her once proudly held head lying motionless in the grass.

Steven has won, she thought dully. He knew how much the life of that animal had meant to her, and yet he had coldly and callously destroyed it before her very eyes. Her punishment for her imagined relationship with James hadn't been enough. Instead, he had chosen this method

173

of retaliation, even at the risk of destroying the growing closeness he had found with his daughter.

What irony! She had been drawn to the wounded deer in much the same way she had been drawn to Steven. She had pitied the animal her wounds, admiring the strength she possessed to go on living for the sake of her young, just as she had learned to admire a similar strength in Steven.

Silent sobs wrenched her body in painful spasms as her gaze moved from the still animal toward the approaching destroyer. Shaking her head in horrified rejection, she backed away, one hand pressed tightly against the back of her mouth to stifle a scream. She met his eyes and was trapped—trapped by her wounds as surely as her broken little deer had been.

She didn't remember turning to run. The next thing she knew her feet were flying over the grass, tears blinding her vision. Her frenzied pace quickened as her imagination distorted reality. She sensed rather than heard his relentless pursuit just moments before she was grappled to the ground, the breath knocked out of her lungs.

"You silly little fool," he raged, jerking her limp body against him. "What the hell are you trying to do?

"You killed her," she moaned, pounding his chest with her fists. "She never did anything to hurt you. You're worse than an animal. You're a murderer. A murderer!"

Suddenly she was being shaken with a force that threatened to snap her neck. She was helpless under the assault, and even more helpless to withstand the terrible rage gripping him. Finally he flung her away with an exclamation of disgust, leaving her shaking with reaction as he rose to his feet.

"You don't know what you're saying!"

Drawing in a ragged breath, she glared at him, love

distorted by a loathing disillusion. "I know exactly what I'm saying," she cried. "You hate me, hate me so much you'd use something like this to hurt me. Well, I hope I've given you satisfaction!"

While she was hurling her abusive words at him, his face had become even more implacably grim. A curious flicker showed briefly in his eyes. If she didn't know better, it could almost have been an expression of pain, but when she saw the sneering slash to his mouth, she realized how ridiculous that assumption was. He was too inured within his unapproachable armor to care what she thought of him!

As if to corroborate her reasoning, he turned on his heels and strode purposefully in the direction of the glade. A more horrible thought came to her, and she jumped to her feet. He wouldn't . . .

"You're not going to butcher her," she screamed, her fists clenched at her sides as she approached his kneeling figure. "I won't let you!"

"For God's sake, grow up!" he remarked quietly, running his hands over the deer's flanks with a curiously gentle motion. About ready to strike out at him, she noticed a muscle jump in the animal, and shock stilled her movements.

"She isn't dead," she whispered, turning disbelieving eyes in his direction.

"She's drugged!"

"I—I don't understand."

"You wouldn't," he laughed, and Eden flinched at the harshly uttered mockery. "I'm sorry to disappoint you, but I'm not quite the monster you think me. I knew it would be a miracle for her to survive much longer in this condition. If she wasn't shot during hunting season, she'd be a sitting duck for other animals. The authorities will be here shortly to transfer her to a place where she'll receive proper medical attention. If there's anything they can do for her it will be done. If not, she'll be put to sleep. Dawn needn't know the outcome. As far as she's concerned, the deer was patched up and left to roam free. Do you understand?"

Eden nodded, unable to voice her thoughts. She had misjudged him, and guilt flooded through her when she remembered what she had accused him of. With tormented eyes she watched him move away. He returned moments later with a blanket, which he laid carefully over the now heaving body of the barely conscious animal.

"I'm sorry," she whimpered, biting her lip when he turned furious eyes in her direction.

"Don't be," he snapped, his eyes glinting with a dislike he made no attempt to hide. "It's only what I should have expected, coming from you."

"That's not fair," she protested. "You've often said the animal should be put out of her misery. What was I supposed to think when I saw you shoot her?"

To her surprise he nodded affirmatively, getting to his feet slowly. His head was bowed, his hand rubbing the muscles of his neck tiredly.

"You're right," he admitted quietly. "I didn't see you, or I would have waited until later. Another day wouldn't have mattered, since I've waited this long."

"Why did you wait until now?"

Her question was gentle, a wealth of tenderness blossoming inside of her for this reserved, often stern man, whose inner goodness was too often hidden beneath a deceptive harshness. She had known this intuitively from the very beginning, the recent emotional frustrations of her growing vulnerability where he was concerned blinding her to the truth. She loved him!

Again she had run true-to-form, she thought bitterly. She was an emotional coward, unable to risk further rejection by showing her feelings. A new determination grew in her as she listened to him explain his delay in getting help for the deer. She should have guessed, should have known that he had been concerned about the young fawn, which had needed the time to learn survival.

"If we had taken the mother earlier, her offspring would have lost his instinctive fear of man. He deserved a chance to run free and wild, as God intended," he said.

"Oh, Steven," she whispered, laying a shaking hand on his shoulder. "I'm sorry, so sorry. I know it doesn't matter to you, but you have to realize I wouldn't deliberately cause you pain, even though I've . . ." Her voice faltered as she struggled to reach him, but she mustered all of her willpower for a last attempt. "Oh, Steven! I can't hide my feelings from you any longer. You deserve to know that I love—"

"You're right!" He rose to his feet, and began moving away from her touch with a swiftness that smacked of revulsion. "It doesn't matter! You were right in the first place. Our marriage has been a disaster from start to finish, and the sooner you take steps to rectify it, the better. Don't worry," he muttered, turning to once again bend over the deer. "We can manage to share Dawn between us, if nothing else."

Her hand dropped to her side. She'd tried and failed, she thought bitterly, as she walked sluggishly back to the house. He didn't need her, and now he didn't even desire her. At least she'd been spared the humiliation of finishing her sentence, she thought. How much lower her self-esteem would have been if she'd already admitted her love for him!

Eden didn't know how she survived the torment of the next hours as she lay dry-eyed, unable to envision a life without Steven. Even tears were denied her as she lay in her own private hell, unable to rouse herself sufficiently to begin the packing she knew she must do. Dawn would have to be told, and although she knew it would hurt her, she didn't think the blow of her stepmother's departure would be as crippling as it once might have been. She now had her father and was secure in his love for her, as well as the new friends she had made. Eventually, if they saw each other occasionally, she would adjust as other children had to learn to live with the parents they loved being apart.

"Mrs. Lassiter." Mrs. Adams's voice came from the hallway. "Mr. Lassiter would like to see you in his study."

"Tell him I—I've got a headache," she replied, not able to stand the thought of facing him again so soon.

"I'm afraid it's urgent," Mrs. Adams replied.

"All right. I'll be there right away," she cried, her earlier indolence superseded by anxiety. *Could something have happened to Dawn?* Dear Lord, she'd be willing to endure Purgatory if only the gravity in Mrs. Adams's voice had been misplaced.

Bursting into the study scant moments later, Eden stopped abruptly, a look of stupefaction on her face. James was there, and beside him stood a petite blonde in a ruched, powder blue pantsuit. She was clinging to his arm, a look of adoration on her face as she looked up at him.

"James," Eden groaned breathlessly, closing her eyes briefly in an excess of relief. "From the way Mrs. Adams sounded, I thought something was wrong."

178

James's grin slashed his face, his eyes twinkling irrepressibly as Eden approached them shyly.

"I'm sorry you got a fright, love," he laughed, "but I wanted you to meet Susan." Looking down at his fianceé he teased, "Honey, this is the other love of my life. The name Eden fits her, because that's just about what she's been to me this last couple of months while you drew out my agony."

Susan turned to Eden, her softly curved mouth tilting upward in pleasure.

"Thank you for what you've done for James," she murmured, reaching out to grasp Eden's hand. "He's talked so much about you that I feel I almost know you."

Eden smiled, shaking her head. "Congratulations, both of you. I'm only glad there's finally a woman brave enough to take James on," she teased. "He can be an exasperating devil at times. I'm relieved that there'll be someone to keep him too busy to get into trouble from now on," she chuckled, her own laughter merging with Susan's. "I've got to admit that he's been rather wearing on my nerves lately."

"Now wait just a minute," James protested. "Eden's been mother enough. Don't you two start joining forces. I'll be wearing the pants in this family, thank you!"

Eden's laughter was abruptly stilled when Steven's voice sounded from behind her.

"I'd like to add my congratulations to my wife's."

Her face blanching, Eden spun around, only realizing at that moment that he must have been standing in the back of the room the whole time. She would have noticed if he had entered through the door.

Silently she stared at him, noticing the strange glitter in his eyes with a sinking sensation in the pit of her stomach. She felt confused by his piercing glance, and a slow flush replaced her earlier pallor. His smile spoke volumes, and was for her alone. The blood pounded through her veins, causing the breath to catch in her throat. His eyes moved briefly to the furiously throbbing pulse point in her throat before returning to her face, his look one of brooding deliberation.

Desperate to avoid his perusal, she turned toward James and Susan, chattering with forced gaiety. James was at his maddening best. His eyes would wander from her to Steven with meaningful intent, his conversation punctuated with such blatant innuendos that Eden had great difficulty in restraining herself from hitting him over the head with something.

"James and I are going to celebrate our engagement tonight," Susan smiled, giving James's arm a meaningful squeeze when she noticed the growing tension in Eden's face. "We would be happy if you and Steven would agree to come."

"Oh, I don't think—"

"We'd be glad to accept," Steven interrupted, a mocking smile increasing Eden's discomforture, "wouldn't we, honey?"

By the time they were finally seated at the Tail o' the Whale restaurant in Bridge Bay, Eden felt hunted. Desperately she looked out of the large bay windows, flaming torches along the deck outside sending flickering reflections dancing on the glass. In the distance was a large, private boat dock, but she quickly averted her eyes from the craft moored there. The bobbing boats made her think of Steven's cruiser, bringing to mind an incident she would rather not remember!

From the moment Steven had accepted the invitation, she had become little more than a pawn. Although she had glared at him in frustration, there had been very little she could do to get herself out of the arrangements. It would have been churlish to refuse to accompany them, especially with Susan's excited exclamations ringing in her ears. Quickly changing into a cinnamon halter-necked pantsuit which left the lightly tanned expanse of her back bare, she had seethed with resentment, a resentment which had increased until now it had assumed gigantic proportions.

Eden talked and smiled and laughed, joining in the teasing banter around the cleverly designed table that resembled the hatch cover of a ship, complete with knotted ropes. The mellow warmth of the restaurant was a welcome distraction, helping to ease the nervous tension assailing her due to Steven's closeness. He was devastating in his white leisure-wear suit and a shimmering bronze shirt open at the throat showing tantalizing glimpses of softly curling hair.

To her discomfiture, he had moved his captain's chair much too near hers. She was immensely grateful for the widely curving arms that prevented an even closer contact. Even so, he still found the opportunity to caress her neck with subtle movements, and it didn't take much intelligence to guess that he was being deliberately irritating.

She was powerless to stop him without making herself appear ridiculous. Her one attempt to carelessly shrug away his disturbing fingers had been a miserable failure. His hand had slid down the smooth softness of her back to her waist, as if to punish her for her withdrawal. When the probing fingers insinuated themselves an inch or so below the elastic band at the back of her slacks, she turned

181

to freeze him with her stare, only to muffle a shocked gasp when she met the slumbrous suggestiveness in his eyes.

Instantly her mind flew backward in erotic fantasy, her thoughts replacing the tantalizing touch of his fingers with warm, moist, seeking lips. A taunting grin showed her that he, too, shared the memory. By the time he withdrew his hand, she was shaking with reaction, all desire to eat the delicious meal in front of her disappearing beneath the embarrassed flush heating her body.

She was never as glad for anything in her life as she was when she was finally home, and able to shut herself securely within her room, but as she showered, James's whispered remark as he left to take Susan to her hotel went round and round in her head.

Don't put him out of his misery too quickly, Eden, he had hissed. *It'll do him good to squirm awhile.*

Wiping the moisture from her body with jerky movements, she couldn't help wondering if the excitement of his engagement had slipped James completely off his trolley. All his interference had caused this evening was a nagging headache along the base of her skull. She took two aspirin from the medicine cabinet, but her hand was shaking so much she could hardly lift the glass of water to her mouth to swallow them. The cool water, however, momentarily alleviated the dryness of her throat. She was the only one squirming, she thought, a bubble of hysteria causing her to choke on the remaining water.

Cotton baby-doll pajamas were her only adornment as she reentered her bedroom. She was very glad for the pink and white childishness of the garment as she halted in the doorway, unaware of the innocent allure her small, daintily curved body presented to the appreciative gaze of the fiery-haired man across the room.

Eden felt her skin prickle with resentment; her lips clamped together in curved reproach. She had known she would find him here eventually, and now the moment she had dreaded all evening had materialized.

"What are you doing here?"

Eden didn't back away from his approaching figure. She had done enough running, she reasoned, tilting her head proudly.

"What do you want me to do?"

She met his intent gaze without flinching, even though the deeply caressing timbre of his voice made her want to flee.

"I want you to leave," she retorted, her chin raised belligerently. "Since I'll be traveling back to Los Angeles tomorrow, I'll need all the rest I can get."

"Like hell you will!"

"You have nothing to do with my decision," she lied, her eyes flickering but managing to remain steadily locked on his. "Although if I remember rightly, the idea was yours in the first place."

"That was when I was sure I was going to hear you confess to being in love with James. I wish now that I'd let you finish your sentence this afternoon in the glade. Why didn't you tell me about Susan?"

"You've never given me the chance to tell you about anything," she remarked tiredly, shaking her head and walking away from him to stand staring sightlessly in her dressing table mirror. "Oh, I know there've been times when you've wanted to make love to me, but you've never wanted to know me, really know me," she sighed, picking up the brush in front of her and fingering it absently.

"Eden, do you love me? Was that what you were trying to tell me?"

He had moved to stand directly behind her, and there was nothing she could do to prevent him from seeing the raw agony that creased her features. Dear God, she agonized. Why did he have to ask her that? Hadn't he punished her enough? Did he have to make her pay for being a woman over and over again?

When she didn't answer, his hands went to her shoulders, turning her as easily as if she were a rag doll. The exquisite pleasure of his touch made her tremble, and she had to bite down on the soft fullness of her lip to stop herself from screaming out her feelings.

"Please," she whimpered, staring at him in hopeless longing. "Please, leave me something. You've t-taken everything else, and I—I just can't fight you anymore."

"Then don't fight me," he coaxed, moving his hands and beginning to untie the strings holding her top in place. "Just love me, honey, and let me love you."

She felt as if the following moments were happening to someone else. She offered no resistance as he stripped the clothing from her body and then slowly removed his own garments. She was numb, his request to allow him to love her beguiling her into a state of mindless reciprocation. He didn't mean the words the way she so desperately needed him to mean them, but she was past caring. All that mattered was this drowning ecstasy as he moved the enveloping hardness of his body against her, the moist, slippery warmth of clinging mouths and thrusting tongues.

He couldn't seem to bear to lose contact with her softly willing flesh, grasping her waist tighter in urgent demand. As he lifted her, her toes brushed gently against his straining calves when he carried her toward the bed. Her emotions rocketed into moaning supplication as his lips moved to her breast, the dampened glide of his tongue causing her

184

to clutch at his hair in an effort to draw more of herself inside the willing cavern.

Their rasping breaths joined forces with the wind rustling through the trees, the soft swishing of writhing bodies against ruffled satin adding a new cadence to the symphony of their joining.

Eden could no longer hold back. The burning thrust of his body as he plundered the very depths of her womanhood transmitted its fire to her mind. There was only the need within her to give and receive, and give yet again, in a never-ending sequence of eternal splendor. The only meaningful reality left was in trembling bodies drawing deeper together, until the very force of life itself was sought and captured in timeless pleasure, which left Eden sobbing as the blazing rapture finally exploded in her brain.

For endless moments she rested against his sweat-moistened body, inhaling the clean, salty scent of his skin with delight. Turning her head, her mouth gently caressed his neck, feeling his arm tighten around her as he drew her closer against his side.

"God, it was good," he muttered against her hair. "You pack quite a punch in that small body of yours."

She moved her cheek over the hair on his chest in a kittenish movement, delighting in the feel of it against her skin.

"Eden?"

"Mmmm?" Her answering murmur was almost absent-minded, her fingers now burrowing themselves within the furry down.

"You never did answer my question."

Eden stiffened. She didn't want to talk, didn't want to say anything to shatter her wonderful tranquility. She suddenly resented the man against whose body she rested, this beloved but unloving man she had married so unwillingly. He was once again ripping her peace from her, forcing her to return to reality.

A recurrence of her earlier agony pierced her, and she jumped to her feet. She grabbed a folded afghan from the foot of the bed, wrapped it around her, and stepped onto the patio. She needed to escape from the walls that had so briefly provided her with paradise. Slow tears trickled down her cheeks for the lost beauty of what she had shared so briefly with the man she loved.

"Eden, don't," he groaned, wrapping his arms around her in the darkness and pulling her against him.

"I—I can't help it," she muttered, attempting to move from his constricting arms, only to have them tighten inexorably.

"I don't blame you," he murmured, his mouth brushing her hair aside and finding her neck. "I've given you no reason to love me, but if you'll give me the chance, I promise things will be different. From the first moment I saw you standing at my door, your doe-soft eyes both hopeful and apprehensive, I knew you meant trouble. There was nowhere I could go to escape the warmth of your loving. It was there, all around me, until I almost hated you for making me feel again. When I thought you were in love with James, I wanted to kill you—anything to save myself from falling further under your spell. Instead, I found myself seeking forgetfulness in your body, at least until you started crying. God," he groaned, his large form shaking with remembered anguish. "I thought you wanted James, and I suddenly loved you too much to take you when I knew you loved him. Sending you away from me was like ripping the heart from my body, Eden."

She remained still as his voice faded into the night. Almost like a benediction the rising sun began to appear on the horizon. Shadows lifted, and she could vaguely see the sun glistening on the distant water of the lake. Curving her arms over his, she nestled against him, the caressing movement of her head causing him to gasp audibly.

"Eden, please," he groaned, his mouth moving feverishly against her hair.

"I love you," she whispered achingly. "I'll always love you."

Turning her head to plunder the depths of the tenderness alight in his eyes, she smiled briefly before once again moving to greet the new day. Now the beautiful, snowcapped reflection of Mount Shasta was in the startlingly blue depths of the lake. For her, the mountain would forever be a symbol of new life, dispelling the loneliness of the past. Like a gentle blessing, the twilight over Eden was at last lifted, and her soul leaped to meet the dawn as she turned to bask in the warmth of Steven's love.

LOOK FOR NEXT MONTH'S
CANDLELIGHT ECSTASY ROMANCES™

When You Want A Little More Than Romance—

Try A Candlelight Ecstasy!